TOTALLY
UNEXPECTED!

TOTALLY UNEXPECTED!

P. C. MAGNUSSEN

REDEMPTION
PRESS

Written & Illustrated by P. C. Magnussen
Cover Design by Brittany Osborn

Published by Redemption Press, PO Box 427, Enumclaw, WA 98022
Toll Free (844) 2REDEEM (273-3336)

Redemption Press is honored to present this title in partnership with the author. The views expressed or implied in this work are those of the author. Redemption Press provides our imprint seal representing design excellence, creative content and high quality production.

All Bible quotations in this story were taken from *The New King James Bible*, copyright 1979, Thomas Nelson, Inc. Publishers, Nashville, Tennessee.

ISBN 13: 978-1-63232-776-5 (Print)
         978-1-63232-777-2 (ePub)
         978-1-63232-779-6 (Mobi)

Library of Congress Catalog Card Number: 2016944397

Dedication

This story is dedicated to Shelley, Sandra, and Amber,
who helped in its completion.

CHAPTER 1

The Park

It was late March. Rebecca felt Butch's massive muscular arm drape across her shoulders as she retrieved her math and science books from her locker at Whatcom High School. She quickly shoved off his arm, slammed the locker shut, and turned to face him. He placed his arms against the wall on either side of her, pinning her, and then leaned in.

"Let's go to Rick's for some burgers after school today, and later we can go to a movie at the Bijou and then . . ." Butch's tone of voice demanded rather than invited.

"And why would I want to do that? I'm *not* your girlfriend," Rebecca replied.

"Because it's only natural that the best athlete at Whatcom High School goes out with the most popular and most beautiful girl; it's your destiny."

"Butch, I appreciate the attention, I really do, but I'm *never* going out with you."

"You'd better meet me after school at Rick's or else!"

"Or else what? What part of *never* don't you understand? I'm going to be late for class." Rebecca ducked under his arm.

"You'd better be there!" Butch grabbed her upper arm.

"Let go of me, Butch!"

"Is there a problem here?" Mr. Steele the Vice Principal asked as he made his way toward them. "You two had better get to class."

Butch released Rebecca's arm, and she dashed into her science class. She took her seat next to her best friend, Loretta, at one of the lab benches just as the final bell rang.

"Cutting it kind of close, Miss Robinson," Mrs. Goodman, the science teacher, said.

"Sorry, Mrs. Goodman."

Mrs. Goodman turned back to the others. "Okay, listen up class. Today we'll be doing the experiment on electrolysis at the end of chapter twelve. For those of you who read that chapter last night, this should be no problem. Just follow the instructions and be sure to write all of your observations in your lab notebooks. I will be collecting them for grading at the end of class."

"That Neanderthal Butch cornered me at my locker just before class," Rebecca turned and whispered to Loretta. "Can you believe it? He thinks I'm his property. He expects me to meet him at Rick's Diner today after school."

Rebecca and Loretta collected all the equipment they would need for their experiment from the storage cabinets and returned to their seats.

"Here, fill this beaker and these test tubes up with water while I get the electrodes ready. This is going to be fun producing hydrogen and oxygen gas from just water," Rebecca said.

"Maybe for a science geek like you, but I don't see anything fun about this," Loretta said.

"I know what Butch wants. He just wants to hook up with me so he can add another notch to his belt! Well, that's not going to happen. If any guy wants this," Rebecca pointed to her body, "he's going to have to put a ring on my finger first."

"Butch is a little rough around the edges, but I think he's cute." Loretta flipped her curly red locks out of the way.

"Yeah, Butch is a fine physical specimen, but I would not call a narcissistic control freak like him cute." Rebecca clamped the test tubes and electrodes in place.

"He's not the only control freak around here," Loretta muttered under her breath as she handed a large beaker full of water to Rebecca.

"What was that?" Rebecca asked.

"Oh . . . nothing. I'd go out with Butch if he asked me."

"If you like him so well, you can have him. Maybe *you* should meet Butch at Rick's. That would be a big help to me because there's no way I'm going to Rick's to be with Butch. I want a guy who will treat me with respect and love *me* and not just my body. I want to find true love and have a future away from this small town. And, eventually, have a family of my own."

"Me too. I want all that, but for now, I would love to have a boyfriend. I'll be happy to keep Butch busy after school."

"Good. I'll slip away to our meadow at Lake Whatcom Park and meet you there later."

"Yes, I'll make up some excuse to leave Butch. I can even sneak some of my dad's beer for us. After all, it's Friday, so we can party at the meadow tonight," Loretta whispered.

"That would be great! I'll pick up some snacks."

After school, while Loretta kept Butch occupied, Rebecca grabbed her pink backpack and headed for the park on her pink mountain bike. She stopped at a sandwich shop to buy two sub sandwiches, still thinking of Butch's "invitation."

"Animals! All the guys at school are nothing but animals! And Butch is the worst!" Rebecca exclaimed to herself as a squirrel darted across the street in front of her. It was a gorgeous sunny day—a rare occurrence in early spring for Whatcom, Washington. The fresh mountain air caressed her cheeks and blew the long blond hair flowing from beneath her pink bicycle helmet back behind her, like an old time aviator's scarf. She pedaled up to the edge of the forest at Lake Whatcom Park. Rebecca liked the meadow there because it was surrounded by the forest. She and Loretta had discovered it when they'd first explored the park ten years earlier. They'd been in the first grade then. Rebecca didn't care what her parents thought about her and Loretta hanging out at the meadow that evening. She was nearly seventeen and felt she could make her own decisions now that she was almost an adult. Besides, there wasn't much else to do in Whatcom. She'd already seen the movie currently playing at the Bijou.

Rebecca knew her good looks made every guy in school want to date her. She could see their yearning as she walked down the hallway. But she knew they had only one thing on their minds; they just wanted to hook up with her. And, of course, all the girls either hated her or wanted desperately to be her friend so they would be elevated socially by such an association. Although Rebecca enjoyed the attention, she tried very hard not to let it go to her head.

Rebecca carefully walked her bike down a path which led into the woods, pushing past the lush ferns cowering beneath the towering fir trees. She breathed in the fresh smell of the woods. It was peaceful there. All she could hear was the occasional twitter of birds. As she approached the meadow, the glint of the sun reflected intensely off of something in the meadow. Rebecca stashed her bike, backpack, and helmet next to a large tree in the ferns. She continued down the path to the meadow—and froze. She didn't know whether to stay put or to run.

What's this? A UFO in the middle of the meadow? The strange craft looked like a giant black triangle about fifty feet long with a wingspan of about sixty feet from end to end. There were windows on the top of what seemed to be a cockpit. She half expected little green men to pop out and zap her with their ray guns. She didn't see anyone, however, so she cautiously crept up for a closer look. *I've got to check this thing out.*

Rebecca smelled lingering smoke from the scorch marks in the grass. They were directly below six small openings in the bottom of the UFO; she noticed them as she walked under it. The UFO was about six feet off the ground, resting on rubber tires that extended from it like the landing gear of an airliner, only smaller. In the middle of the craft, by the main landing gear, extended a small ladder that came from the interior of the UFO. At one end of the "wing", some panels were open, exposing the inside. A tool box rested on the ground near a small step ladder. Where had the occupants of the UFO gone? And where did they get these ordinary tools? Did these aliens steal them from someone's garage?

Rebecca explored the open panels. She paused at the base of the ladder. Perhaps it wouldn't hurt to take a quick peek inside. *After all, I could use a little adventure in my life. I would love to know more about this UFO and what makes it tick.* She climbed the ladder through the wheel well leading into an open hatch in the floor. Rebecca cautiously raised her head above the floor of the cockpit. There was no one inside. The coast was clear. At first glance, the flight compartment was disappointing. There were just four ordinary looking seats; two in front of a massive instrument panel and two more behind them. Rebecca crawled up into the cabin. Behind her—towards the back of the flight deck—were various sizes of lockers suitable for holding equipment. Rebecca walked towards the instrument panel and noticed all the labels were written in English. *That's strange you would think aliens would use some exotic language.* She peered out the windows. There was nothing but trees in front of her.

Rebecca heard voices outside. *Oh, perfect! They've returned! I'm so freaking dead!* She crept down the ladder and lowered her head below the opening to get a look at the source of the conversation. She started to sneak down the ladder to get away but thought better of it. *What if they see me?* The two men in spacesuits had reached the open access panels. One was up on the step ladder, reaching in to work inside the aircraft, and the other stood on the ground with his back towards her, handing up tools.

"It's a good thing we're close to home so we could get some spare parts, Dad," said the one on the ground.

"Yes, otherwise we would really be in trouble. I'm glad we found this meadow, too. This way, we can land without people seeing us. The last thing we need is undue attention—especially from industrial spies."

These guys don't look or sound like aliens. Maybe they're just humans?

"Alright, the new component is in place; go power things up. Let's see if it's going to work, Scott."

"Okay, Dad." The one called Scott turned and walked toward the ladder Rebecca sat on.

Rebecca jerked her head up, scrambling up the ladder while frantically looking for a place to hide. She opened the largest locker. More space suits! She climbed inside and closed the door behind her. She left just enough of space so she could peek through a crack at the instrument panel. Rebecca sat on the floor, her back against the wall, her legs scrunched up but still touching the front wall. The spare flight suits hanging above her draped over the top of her. No sooner was she hidden inside than the man referred to as Scott came quickly up the ladder and bounded towards the instrument panel. All Rebecca could see was his back as he turned on some switches, which caused the entire aircraft to hum like a hive of bees waking from a nap.

"Okay Dad, everything checks out," Scott said over the radio. "It looks like we're good to go."

"Good! We need to get out of here. We've already lost too much time. Come help me button things up."

As Scott turned to leave the cockpit, Rebecca instinctively turned away from the crack.

"That's odd, why is this locker door open?" Scott firmly closed the door and climbed back down the ladder.

Rebecca was now in complete darkness. She felt around the door for a latch to open it from the inside. Nothing! She was trapped.

Panic spread throughout her body. What could she do? What would these guys do to her if they found her in their UFO? Would she ever see her family again? She pulled out her cell phone to call for help. Its light permeated the locker, but... no service! Frantically, she moved her phone around the locker to find a signal. Still no service! Tears trailed down her cheeks as Rebecca tried to summon courage. How could she explain this to these guys, or to her parents if she ever saw them again? *I'm done for; I'm so totally done for.*

Soon, the two men climbed the ladder and entered the cockpit. There was a clatter of locker doors closing as they stowed the equipment. She heard the hatch in the floor close with a thump. There was a roar of rocket engines beneath her, and she sensed the aircraft rising into the sky, like a very fast elevator might. It stopped and hovered for a few seconds. She heard the hum of the landing gear being raised and felt the doors close. Her back began to vibrate against the locker wall. The two jet engines in the back were deafening as they throttled up but then they quieted to a dull hum. The UFO shot forward and up at a steep angle, causing Rebecca to bang her head on the back wall of the locker which caused a loud boom. She rubbed the back of her head to relieve the excruciating pain, wanting to scream, but she didn't dare. The UFO leveled out, but there was still a sensation of moving forward.

Rebecca heard footsteps and the clanging of locker doors opening and closing. The door to the locker where she was hiding burst open, and the light from the cockpit blasted her eyes. When Scott pulled back the flight suits to get a better look inside, Rebecca stiffened. She stared up in horror at the man before her in a white spacesuit with a dark visor pulled down on his helmet.

"Whoa, Dad! There's a girl hiding in the locker where we store the flight suits," Scott said over the microphone in his helmet.

"A girl?" the dad yelled.

"Yes, a girl."

"They'll do anything to find you, Scott, won't they?"

"Alright, Dad!" Scott laughed.

"How did she get in there?"

"Well Dad, if I knew, you'd know."

"Good point, Son, she must have climbed in while we were picking up the spare part from Daniel. Well, it's too late to turn back now. We don't have the time or the fuel to spare to take her back. She'll just have to come with us. Get her into a flight suit, Scott so that we can get back underway."

Scott raised the dark visor on his helmet and extended his hand to Rebecca. "Hi, I'm Scott. What's your name?"

"R-r-r-r-becca R-r-r-robinson," Rebecca stammered as she looked up at Scott's kind blue eyes.

"We need to get you out of there and into a flight suit for your own safety."

"Are you aliens? Please don't hurt me," Rebecca pleaded.

"We're not aliens, but our true home is not of this world, and we wouldn't dream of hurting you. Now, please take my hand and come out of there."

Rebecca grasped his gloved hand and gingerly climbed out of the locker. Her legs and feet tingled as the blood rushed back into them. Scott grabbed one of the flight suits from the locker.

These guys may not be so bad after all. They may not kill me, but my parents will when they find out what happened. Hmmm, Scott's not bad looking.

"This is my mom's suit. I think it will fit you, Rebecca. Place your hands on my shoulders and I will help you climb into it."

Rebecca grasped Scott's muscular shoulders as he pulled the flight suit over her sneakers, blue jeans, and pink shirt. After she zipped up the suit, he gently placed the gloves over her hands, making sure everything was properly sealed. Then he took a helmet from the locker and placed it over her head, locking it in place on the suit's collar after she tucked her long hair out of the way. Scott turned some knobs on the front of the suit, and Rebecca heard the crackle of the radio speakers in her helmet come on. He closed the locker door, took Rebecca's hand, and led her to the seat behind his dad. After she had sat down, Scott fastened the safety harness around her, activated the ejector mode switch on the seat, and hooked up a hose to her suit. She felt the rush of cool air inside. Scott pulled down her visor and took his seat again.

"Rebecca, this is my dad, Ashley Anderson. Dad, this is Rebecca Robinson."

"You have a lot of nerve young lady, stowing away on our plane. Don't you have any respect for other people's property?" Mr. Anderson scolded.

"I'm sorry, sir, my curiosity got the better of me. I didn't like expect to find a UFO in the meadow. What are you going to do with me?"

"We forgive you, Rebecca," Mr. Anderson said. "And for your information, this is *not* a UFO. It's an experimental aircraft built by my company, Anderson Aerospace, called the AX-44. As for you, you'll just have to come with us to Hawaii where we're going to pick up my wife. When we get there, you can call your parents and explain what happened. I imagine they'll be worried sick. We'll bring you home Saturday."

"Oh no! My best friend Loretta was supposed to meet me at the park. She'll think I was kidnapped! And when my parents find out what happened, I'll be grounded for life!"

"I don't think it will be that bad. Do you live in Whatcom, Rebecca?" Scott asked.

"Yes, my dad owns the sporting goods store there."

"We live there, too, but I don't get to town much."

"Sit back and relax Rebecca, we have a long flight ahead." Mr. Anderson pulled back on the stick, causing the aircraft to shoot up at a steep angle again. He leveled the aircraft off and banked towards the southwest.

"Set a course for Hawaii, Scott, on the navi-computer," Mr. Anderson said as he throttled up the jet engines to full power.

"Right, Dad, course locked in."

"Mr. Anderson, I was wondering what the skin of this aircraft is made of?" Rebecca asked. "It felt like a ceramic vase."

"You're not far off Rebecca. It's a ceramic composite material we invented called Ceracite. It helps protect the aircraft from the heat of traveling at supersonic speeds and is lighter than aluminum."

Rebecca gazed out the window. She could barely see the ground below through the clouds. It looked like they were coming up on North Seattle. She had never flown in an airplane before and found the whole experience exhilarating. *Are these guys really who they say they are? Can I trust them?* She dreaded telling her parents what had happened. What must they and Loretta think about her sudden disappearance?

CHAPTER 2

The Missed Meeting

After she had ditched Butch at Rick's, Loretta rode her red mountain bike up to the forest at Lake Whatcom Park, her red backpack jostling back and forth with each stroke of the bike pedals. She could hear the beer bottles clinking together on the bottom of the backpack. *Let's get this party started.* As she walked her bike up the path to the meadow, she noticed Rebecca's pink bike propped against a large fir tree. Loretta placed her bike there, too, along with her red bike helmet.

"Rebecca! Where are you?" Silence. Then, only the sound of a few birds chattering in the trees.

"Rebecca! I'm here. Come on; this isn't funny. I brought the beer. It's still cold."

Still nothing. Loretta took out her cell phone and texted Rebecca, but got no response. Now Loretta was worried. She pulled a bottle of beer from her backpack and looked in Rebecca's backpack. "Oh, good! She brought some sub sandwiches." Loretta sat on the ground and ate the sandwich and drank the beer while she pondered what to do next. No sense letting the food go to waste.

What if somebody had kidnapped Rebecca? It wasn't like her friend just to leave her things and run off. After looking around the woods and the meadow for over an hour, she called the rest of the cheer squad to help find Rebecca, too. With no success, Loretta finally decided she'd better call Rebecca's father. It was almost six o'clock.

"Robinson residence." Mr. Robinson said.

"Hey Mr. Robinson, this is Loretta. Rebecca was supposed to meet me at the park after school, but I can't find her. Her bike and stuff are here, but she's like—nowhere. I tried texting her but got nothing. I have a bad feeling something happened to her."

"Loretta you stay right there. I'll get the sheriff, and we'll be there in a few minutes."

Dark shadows crept across the meadow as the sun ducked behind the trees. After what seemed like forever, Loretta heard two men's voices and saw two flashlights bouncing up the path. She hid until she was sure it was safe, quickly tossing the empty beer bottle into the ferns.

"Loretta! We're here, come on out," Mr. Robinson said. "Look Bud, here are the girls' bikes."

Loretta dashed out from her hiding place and threw her arms around Mr. Robinson. "I was so scared."

"Get your things, honey, and I'll take you home," Mr. Robinson said. "I'm sure Sheriff Brown will figure out why Rebecca is missing."

Loretta followed with her bike down the path to the parking lot as Mr. Robinson pushed Rebecca's bike to his red Ford Bronco. After they had loaded everything into the back, they returned to the meadow to see if Sheriff Brown found any clues to Rebecca's disappearance.

"What have you discovered, Bud?" Mr. Robinson asked. "Do you have any idea what happened to my daughter?"

"Ralph, see where the grass is mashed down between each set of these scorch marks? It looks like something very heavy was parked here. Also, look over here." Bud aimed his flashlight towards the end of the meadow. "See in the grass; there are four small impressions. It appears they were using a small step ladder. And here are some pieces of stripped-off plastic insulation I found." He waved a small plastic evidence bag. "It looks like a large aircraft landed here for repairs and then left, perhaps taking your daughter with them. I've heard reports about a UFO leaving the park in a cloud of smoke and fire this afternoon. One guy even sent me this photo from his cell phone." He pulled out his phone and shared the picture. "Have you ever seen anything like that? It looks like a UFO from one of those TV shows. Ralph, I think your daughter was abducted by aliens!"

Loretta looked at the photo on the sheriff's phone in disbelief. "I'll never see my BFF again!" she sobbed.

"Nonsense. I'm sure there's a logical explanation for all of this," Mr. Robinson said. "I wonder if it could be the Andersons? We often hear their aircraft taking off and landing out at their estate."

"That's certainly a possibility," Bud said. "I'll give the Andersons a call. Meanwhile, I'm going to take some photos of the scene. We'll get to the bottom of all this, Ralph. Now why don't you two go home; I'll be in touch."

Loretta and Mr. Robinson trudged back to his Bronco, and he began driving home.

"How am I going to break the news to Elaine that our little girl is missing?" Mr. Robinson said. "I hate to admit it but Rebecca is my favorite child. I love her so much, and now she may be gone forever."

"And what am I going to do without my best friend?" Loretta cried. "I love her, too."

"Try not to panic yet. I have to believe that Rebecca will be alright. I'll let you know if there's any news, Loretta." Ralph Robinson parked in his driveway and unloaded the bikes.

"Thanks, Mr. Robinson." Loretta rode her bike across the street to her garage. She rushed inside her house and ran upstairs to her room. After stashing the rest of the beer in her closet, she flopped on her bed and drowned her pillow with tears.

"What's wrong, honey?" Betty Flannigan stood in the doorway to Loretta's room.

"Rebecca's missing." Loretta sat up on her bed and wiped her freckled, tear-drenched face with her hands. "My best friend in all the world is gone, Mom!"

Mrs. Flannigan sat down on the bed to comfort her daughter. Then she must have smelled beer on Loretta's breath.

"Have you been drinking your father's beer again? What have we told you about this? Just wait until your father gets home, young lady."

"Mom, don't judge me! My best friend has been kidnapped—or worse—and all you can talk about is my drinking some of Dad's beer! Besides, I don't know what the big deal is. It was just one beer."

"It *is* a big deal, Loretta! As a minor, you're not allowed to drink alcohol. If the police caught you, we could all be in trouble. Your dad and I will discuss your punishment and let you know in the morning. Meanwhile, I'm sorry about your friend." Betty Flannigan rubbed her daughter's back. "Does the sheriff have any idea what happened? Can I get you some hot chocolate and cookies? Would that make you feel better?"

"Sheriff Brown thinks Rebecca was abducted by aliens in a UFO that was parked in the meadow. He even showed us a photo someone sent him. I don't think anything can make me feel better, but some hot chocolate *and* a hot fudge sundae would be wonderful. What am I going to do Mom? Things just won't be the same without Rebecca."

"Give it time, honey. I'll go fix some hot chocolate and ice cream for you."

Mrs. Flannigan left and returned a few minutes later with a tray. She sat on the bed next to her daughter while they both drank hot chocolate and ate hot fudge sundaes.

"I've heard chocolate is an excellent anti-depressant. It's just the thing for such sad news," Mrs. Flannigan said.

"It must be working because I'm feeling a little better," Loretta said. "I remember the first day I met Rebecca like it was yesterday. We both had just started kindergarten and Butch and his friends were teasing me about my red hair. Rebecca stepped in and stood up to them. She said my hair was beautiful. After that, we were like friends for life. Rebecca gave me the courage to be myself."

"Yes, Rebecca was pretty fearless. Honey, remember the time you got your kite stuck up in a tree, and Rebecca just climbed up and got it? And then there's the time you two found an injured Robin and she nursed it back to health. I swear if Rebecca's parents would let her, she'd have a whole zoo. I'm glad they drew the line at just a dog. Too bad he got killed by a car. I'm just glad you girls were at school when it happened. At least she didn't have to see the mess."

"Rebecca loved that dog so much I think she cried for a week. She still loves animals but hasn't quite gotten over Barney's death. She just can't bring herself to get another dog. And she's smart, too, Mom. Because of Rebecca, I was able to get better grades in school. I know I'll never be as smart as she is, but I would have had much worse grades if Rebecca hadn't encouraged me. Yeah, she can be kind of bossy, but it was always for my own good. Oh Mom, I'm really going to miss Rebecca if she doesn't come back."

"Honey, I know it won't be easy, but if Rebecca is really gone, you'll make new friends. You might even meet a nice guy like I did when I met your father."

"I would love to have a boyfriend. I'm kind of crushing on Sheriff Brown's son Butch right now."

"Oh, honey, please don't date him! I've heard that kid is nothing but trouble. Boys like that will only break your heart. Surely there must be nicer boys at school for you to date."

"They might be nicer, but they aren't as cute or as much fun as Butch. I got to hang out with him at Rick's for an hour after school today. He was expecting Rebecca but got me. I loved bugging him. Rebecca wanted me to distract him so she could go to the meadow. If only I hadn't stayed so long, I might have prevented Rebecca from being kidnapped."

"Or you might have both been abducted! Loretta, you need to find a guy who will treat you right. Butch is not that kind of guy. Yes, he might look good on the outside, but it's what's on the inside that counts in the long run. I married your father not because he's a handsome devil, but because he genuinely cares about *me*. Your dad would lay down his life for us. Now that's the kind of guy we would like to see you date. Right now, young lady, I think you need to get to bed."

"Okay, okay I'll think about it. Good night, Mom. Thanks for the goodies."

"Good night, dear." Mrs. Flannigan kissed her daughter's forehead, took the tray, and left the room.

Loretta got ready for bed and slipped under the covers. She stared into the darkness at the posters of all her favorite boy bands and thought some more about Rebecca. *What is the cheer squad going to do if Rebecca doesn't return?* Rebecca worked out all the choreography for each cheer. *I'd never have had the courage to join without Rebecca encouraging me to do so. And now what can I do for a career if Rebecca doesn't return?* She'd been counting on working with Rebecca to start a catering business. Rebecca was Loretta's only motivation for graduating from high school. She just wanted to party and get Butch to notice her.

Maybe with Rebecca out of the picture, he would. Loretta felt bad for thinking such a thing. She might just have to find a way to get through school and carry on if her friend never came back. After all, she knew a few dance moves the cheer squad could use. Rebecca wasn't the only one who knew how to dance. Loretta thought about all the fun they'd had growing up and began to cry again until she fell asleep.

Then, her cell phone—on the nightstand by her bed—began to vibrate.

CHAPTER 3

The Close Call

"Beep, beep, beep!" After only thirty minutes of flying, Rebecca heard the proximity alarm sound off and saw a red light flash on the instrument panel. *Now, what? Are we going to crash?*

"Uh oh, it looks like we have company!" Mr. Anderson said. "According to the sensors, we have two F-15 fighter planes headed straight for us."

"I'll turn on our transponder so they can see us," Scott said.

"What Scott means, Rebecca, is that this aircraft uses stealth technology so that it is nearly invisible on radar. Unless we turn on our transponder, those jets will collide with us in about thirty seconds."

Scott turned on the transponder, and they all watched the sensor screen as the two blips got closer and closer. Soon after that, through the window, they saw two dark shapes speeding towards them. Scott tuned their radio to the same frequency as the fighter planes.

The two F-15 Eagle fighter jets zoomed above, just missing them by about ten feet.

"Whoa! What was that?" said one of the pilots on the radio.

"According to the transponder data, it's an AX-44," the other pilot replied. "It's an experimental aircraft made by Anderson Aerospace, Eagle Two."

"Roger, Eagle One."

"I think we should get a better look at it, Eagle Two."

"Roger, Eagle One."

Mr. Anderson, Scott, and Rebecca watched the screen as the two blips moved in opposite directions to turn around, forming a heart shape in the sky as they met up again to fly in formation.

"Looks like they're coming back, Dad."

"They're about to get a big surprise. We're almost over the Pacific Ocean, time to go supersonic; fire the two wing rockets, Scott."

As soon as they were over the ocean, Scott pulled back on the throttle levers for the rocket engines, and they shot forward. He then tuned their radios back to their own frequency and switched off the transponder, causing them to disappear from the view of the fighter pilots as they reached Mach 1 in air speed. Rebecca had the sensation of being thrust back into her seat as the aircraft accelerated.

Rebecca soon settled back and watched as the clouds and ocean below streamed under them like a time-lapse video.

"We should arrive at Hawaii in about three hours," Mr. Anderson said. "I think we need some traveling music, Scott. How about a little Beethoven?"

"Okay, the Ninth Symphony coming up." Scott pushed some buttons on the side console.

Rebecca wondered what Loretta and her parents were doing just then, but drifted off to sleep as the soothing tones of classical music filled her ears. She awoke at the sound of radio chatter.

"Lalokai Resort, this is Big Kahuna," Mr. Anderson said. "We're about thirty minutes out from your location. Is the hanger ready?"

"Roger, Big Kahuna," the Lalokai Resort radio operator said. "The hanger's ready. We await your arrival."

Mr. Anderson pushed the stick forward, causing the aircraft to go into a steep dive as Scott shut down the wing rockets, which he said would decrease their air speed. Rebecca could feel her ears pop as they descended to only 1000 feet above the water. Mr. Anderson leveled out the aircraft. He then pushed the jet engine throttle lever forward to reduce their air speed even further.

"Scott, fire the landing rockets and open the ballast tank doors while I lower the aqua jets."

"Preparing to close the intake and exhaust doors on your mark," Scott said. "Landing rockets throttled up. Go ahead and shut down the jets, Dad."

"Jets shut down. Begin our descent Scott; I'm closing all intake and exhaust doors now."

Rebecca looked out the windows and saw only water for miles around them. Why were they landing in the ocean? Was that safe? She felt the aircraft hover over the water and slowly lower towards it. As they got closer to the ocean, she could see a lush green island in front of them on the horizon. She was excited to see what Hawaii would be like.

"It's a good thing we're here, Dad. We're almost out of fuel."

"Brace yourselves everyone," Mr. Anderson said. "It could get a little bumpy once we hit the water; standing by to close the landing rocket doors."

"Okay, cutting the landing rockets in 3 . . . 2 . . . 1 . . . now!" Scott said.

When the rocket engines cut out, Mr. Anderson immediately closed the nozzle doors and the aircraft dropped into the water. After bobbing around for a few seconds, they sank below the surface.

"Taking us down to a depth of 75 feet. Power up the aqua jets, Scott, while I shed some light on the situation." Mr. Anderson switched on the floodlights.

The deep blue water surrounding them was incredibly clear and the flood lights bounced off of the coral and fish in front of them.

Rebecca was relieved they were okay. Still, it seemed strange that they would be going underwater like that. She followed the brightly colored fish darting in front of them as they moved forward. She could see the glow above them, at the ocean's surface. Scott pulled back on the aqua jet throttle, causing the aircraft to speed up as it glided through the water. For what seemed like an eternity, they traveled through the water. Rebecca caught sight of some sea turtles and a shark. This was all so much more exciting than anything she had ever experienced in Whatcom!

Then, she saw some lights in the distance ahead. As they drew closer, it became apparent to Rebecca that there was a massive underwater structure before them, one with several floors, each floor having its own large windows.

"Lalokai, this is the Big Kahuna," Mr. Anderson said. "We're making our final approach. Please open the hanger bay doors."

"Roger, Big Kahuna, opening the hanger doors now," the radio operator said.

Immediately, two huge doors slid open on one end of the structure. Mr. Anderson maneuvered the aircraft over to the opening, lining up the center with a bright yellow stripe running down the middle of the hanger. Scott moved the throttle controls forward to slow down the vehicle. Mr. Anderson carefully inched the AX-44 into the hanger.

As soon as they were safely inside, three pylons unfolded from the floor for the aircraft to rest upon and the hanger doors closed. The water began to drain from the flooded hanger, and the aircraft rested on the pylons. Clamps locked it in place. When all the water had drained from the hanger, a large turntable rotated the aircraft around 180 degrees so that the front faced the hanger door. A ramp extended from the ceiling to a hatch on top of the aircraft.

Mr. Anderson and Scott unfastened their safety harnesses and moved towards the lockers in back. Scott stopped to disarm the ejector modes on their seats and to help Rebecca out of her harness. Mr. Anderson removed his helmet and flight suit, revealing a tall, middle-aged but fit man with graying black hair, dressed in blue coveralls. He opened the hatch above them at the back of the cabin, and two technicians on the ramp lowered a ladder. Meanwhile, Scott helped Rebecca out of her flight suit. First, he removed both their helmets and placed them in the locker.

Rebecca saw Scott's wavy black hair and was greatly impressed by how gentle he was as he helped her out of the flight suit. When he took off his flight suit, she saw he was not only good-looking but in excellent physical shape. Large muscles bulged from beneath his blue coveralls. Like his father, Scott was at least six feet tall. Rebecca was a few inches shorter than him.

Scott and his dad grabbed their overnight bags from a locker, and they all climbed the ladder onto the ramp. As they walked up the ramp, Rebecca followed Mr. Anderson and Scott into a control room at the back of the hanger. There, she saw the man behind the radio voice at the resort. His personnel badge indicated that he was named Mike. He was a young man with sandy brown hair and glasses with a headset on; definitely a nerd if ever she saw one. Rebecca, in spite of her looks, was kind of a nerd, too. She found all of this fascinating.

"Rebecca, you can call your parents now and tell them you're alright," Mr. Anderson said.

Rebecca pulled out her cell phone and was able to get service. She called her home.

"Hello, Robinson residence."

"Hi, Daddy!"

"Rebecca! We were so worried about you! Where are you? What happened?"

"I'm sorry, Dad. I just let my curiosity get the better of me. Please don't be mad. I never meant for any of this to happen. I found what I thought was a UFO in the meadow. While I was exploring it on the inside, I got trapped in one of the lockers. As it turns out, it's really this cool experimental aircraft that had to land for repairs in the meadow. It belongs to Ashley Anderson. We're in Hawaii at his awesome resort. It's like under the sea. He and his son Scott were on their way here to get Mrs. Anderson, and they won't be able to bring me back until sometime tomorrow. They're awfully nice people Dad."

"Rebecca, slow down! What were you thinking going aboard that strange aircraft? I brought your bike and backpack home. We're just glad you're alright. We'll discuss your punishment when you get back. For now, I expect you to be on your best behavior. Please let me talk to Mr. Anderson."

"Okay, Dad I'll put him on, and yes, I'll be good." Rebecca handed Mr. Anderson her phone. "My dad wants to talk to you."

"Hello. Mr. Robinson. This is Ashley Anderson."

"Ashley, I'm awfully sorry for all the trouble Rebecca has caused you. Are you really in Hawaii?"

"Yes, we're near Maui, and your daughter will be fine. We'll bring her back tomorrow."

"Oh good, I was afraid you might have her arrested for stowing away on your plane."

"No, we've forgiven her and have no intention of pressing charges. I hope you won't be too hard on her when she gets back. I have a teenage son, and I know how teens can be. They act before thinking about the consequences."

"Thanks for being so understanding, Ashley. Can I speak with my daughter again?"

Mr. Anderson handed the phone back to Rebecca. "Your dad wants to speak with you some more."

"Hi, Dad. I'm back," Rebecca said.

"You should be grateful Mr. Anderson isn't going to have you arrested for trespassing! Wow! Your Mom will be so jealous. She has always wanted to go to Hawaii. I'd better let you go, Honey. You can tell us all about your big adventure when you get back. It's late here, and I still need to call Bud and let him know you're okay. We love you, kiddo. Good night."

"I love you too, Dad. Goodbye." Rebecca sent a quick text message to her BFF, Loretta, telling her she was okay and was sorry she'd missed their party in the park. Then she put her phone away.

"Now, young lady, if you'll follow us we'll get something to eat and settle you in for the night," Mr. Anderson said.

"Oh good, I'm starved! Also, could you show me to your nearest restroom?"

"Right this way," Scott said as he waved her towards the door.

They walked down a corridor to an elevator which they took up one floor. When the doors opened, they stepped out into a cozy, modern-style living room with plush teal blue carpet, a royal blue sofa and love seat, and thick curved windows all along the outside wall. Fish swam by the windows. Mr. Anderson disappeared down the hall into one of the bedrooms. Scott pointed her in the direction of the bathroom. It was more like they were in a fine hotel and not an undersea facility. When she came out, Scott introduced her to his mom.

"Rebecca, this is my mom, Mary Ann Anderson. She's a marine biologist and is here to check on her research. Mom, this is Rebecca Robinson, our little stowaway," Scott teased.

"Welcome, Rebecca! Aren't you just the prettiest little thing?" Mrs. Anderson gushed in her slight Southern drawl as she embraced Rebecca. "Please make yourself at home. I'll tell the chef to set another place at the table. You must be plumb worn out after such a long trip."

"Thank you, Mrs. Anderson. I'm famished, but too excited to be tired." Rebecca thought the beautiful, slender middle-aged woman before her with shoulder-length blond hair and blue eyes was rather sweet, too.

"Well, come this way, Rebecca, into the dining room. Dinner's almost ready."

They all entered the next room, where there was a long, glass table with stainless steel supports and rounded stainless steel chairs with black padding on the seats. Scott pulled back a chair for Rebecca and sat across from her after she was seated. At Mrs. Anderson's bidding, a man in a chef's outfit emerged from behind a sliding door and put a place-setting in front of Rebecca before dashing back into the kitchen. Rebecca smelled the wonderful aroma of the food they were preparing. She was looking forward to learning more about this family but was a little uneasy being around rich people. Mrs. Anderson took her seat next to the chair at the head of the table. They were soon joined by Mr. Anderson, who was now dressed in a black tuxedo.

"You look pretty spiffy, dear," Mrs. Anderson said as she kissed her husband.

"Thanks, love," he said. "I want to look my best when I speak to our guests next-door. Whenever I'm here, Rebecca, I like to personally greet our guests."

Rebecca nodded. *And where is next-door? Who are these guests?*

After sitting down at the head of the table, Mr. Anderson extended both arms towards Mrs. Anderson and Rebecca and said, "Let's give thanks."

Scott grasped his Mom's hand and reached across the table to take Rebecca's hand. His strong fingers gently clasped her delicate ones. It felt good to have Scott hold her hand.

They all bowed their heads as Mr. Anderson prayed. "Our gracious God and Father, thank you for this food and for bringing us safely together; in Jesus's name, amen."

"I hope you like seafood," Mrs. Anderson said. "Our chef has prepared an excellent Mahi- Mahi this evening, with steamed mixed veggies and wild rice."

"I've never had it, but right now I'm so hungry I could eat an elephant!" Rebecca said.

The chef came out from the kitchen carrying a large serving tray and set before each of them a plate with the fish, vegetables, and rice on it. Rebecca didn't hesitate to begin eating once everyone was served.

"This fish is delicious," she remarked. "My compliments to the chef. I like to cook too and have thought about becoming a chef."

"Thank you, dear, we raise these fish here at this research facility," Mrs. Anderson said. "We have some local species that I am studying and which often find their way onto someone's dinner plate. Part of my research is to find new sources of food that can be raised in captivity to support an undersea habitat. I'm glad you like cooking; so do I. How old are you, Rebecca?"

"I'm sixteen, and your research sounds wonderful."

"What are your favorite classes in school, dear?"

"I like most of my classes, but I think science, math, and swimming are my favorites. I'm on my school's swim team. How old are you, Scott? Where do you go to school?"

"I'm seventeen, and my parents homeschool me with the help of various tutors. Have you ever been scuba diving or snorkeling?" Scott asked.

"No, but I'd love to learn how. I thought this was a resort, not a research facility."

"Actually, it's both," Mr. Anderson said. "Over here in the smaller structure the research facility is housed, and next-door, across the bridge, is the larger structure, our Lalokai Resort. As far as I know, it's the only hotel in the world where all the rooms are underwater."

"After dinner, can I show Rebecca around?" Scott asked.

"I suppose it would be alright," Mr. Anderson said. "Just don't disturb any of our guests or pester the employees. And be back here by ten p.m. We need to get a good night's sleep for our return trip tomorrow."

"Awesome! I'd love to see more of this place!" Rebecca exclaimed. "Mr. Anderson, because this facility is underwater, is that why your aircraft works like a submarine, too?"

"Yes and no, Rebecca. Originally, the AX-44 was just supposed to be a prototype for a supersonic fighter plane, but when we couldn't get the Air Force to buy it, we redesigned it also to serve as a submarine and a spacecraft. About that time, we were developing this resort, too. We use it exclusively for traveling now when it's just our family. Now, if you'll excuse me, I have to greet our guests next-door."

After dinner, Mr. Anderson went next-door to the resort, and Scott ducked into his room to change out of his coveralls while Mrs. Anderson showed Rebecca the guest room. It was a modest bedroom with a large curved window on the outside wall like the rest of their quarters. There were more teal carpet and a queen size bed with a royal blue comforter, on which were laid a white bathrobe and some towels. Off to the side was a small bathroom with a shower.

"Let us know if you need anything," Mrs. Anderson said.

"Do you have a toothbrush I can use?" Rebecca asked.

"Oh yes, you'll find all those things in the medicine cabinet, dear."

Rebecca went into the bathroom to spruce up a bit while Mrs. Anderson turned down her bed.

"What do you think of my son Scott?" she asked.

"He seems like a nice guy. You obviously raised him well."

"Thank you, dear. We tried to make Scott into a true gentleman. Now, where is that boy?"

Rebecca wondered if Scott would want her for a girlfriend. So far, he seemed a lot better than the guys at school—especially Butch. She was excited to spend more time with Scott and to see more of this incredible facility. *What will the resort be like? Will it be just like any other hotel, or different? Is it fancy like these living quarters?*

CHAPTER 4

The Resort

Just then, Scott entered the guest room dressed in blue jeans and a purple Hawaiian shirt. He said, in a stuffy British accent, "Are you ready for your grand tour of the resort, me lady?"

"Oh yes, kind sir," Rebecca giggled. "You look nice, Scott."

"Thanks, I thought we'd start the tour at the research facility and then go over to the resort."

"I'd like that, Scott. I want to see what your mother and her colleagues are doing."

They got back into the elevator and went down to the bottom floor. There, Scott showed Rebecca all the laboratory tanks teeming with fish and other sea creatures. Rebecca thought it was so cool to be able to work with all this sea life. She'd thought about becoming a biologist or a veterinarian so that she could work with animals. But she also wanted to be a chef. She was so confused about what career to pursue. Maybe she could be a chef and help these scientists prepare meals using their undersea food sources.

Scott looked at his watch and exclaimed, "Let's go! If we hurry, we can still catch it."

"Catch what?" Rebecca asked.

"It's a surprise. But trust me, you don't want to miss this."

Rebecca followed Scott back to the elevator, and they went up to the fourth level, where a glass-enclosed bridge spanned the fifty-foot gap between the two structures. Scott straddled a small scooter-like device and told Rebecca to hop on behind him. She sat down on it and placed her arms around Scott's waist. When Scott switched it on, the scooter rose up about an inch off of the floor and hovered in place. Scott pushed a button, and the doors slid open to the bridge. When he turned the throttle, they shot forward onto the bridge. Within seconds, they were across the bridge, and two doors opened in front of them, at the resort, exposing a long glass tunnel. They zoomed to the end of the tunnel, and the scooter stopped automatically. Once inside a large atrium, they climbed off the scooter. Rebecca gazed up at the glass-enclosed elevator and all the different levels above them.

"Whoa, what a rush! What is that thing we just rode on?" Rebecca asked.

"It's a scooter that uses magnetic levitation for propulsion. The staff uses them to move quickly between buildings. The elevators are maglev, too. It's all part of this whole grand experiment in underwater habitats. Come on."

Taking Rebecca's hand, Scott led her around the atrium opening to the elevator, which whisked them to the very top level. From there, Scott waved an access badge over a badge reader and opened a door to a circular stairwell. They hastily climbed to the top, where there was an enclosed vestibule with windows on the front and back, and two doors going outside to their left and to their right, with windows in them, too. Scott directed her to the window facing northwest and said, "Feast your eyes on that."

Rebecca looked out the window and gazed at the most beautiful sunset she had ever seen. The horizon was filled with orange, yellow, and purple hues as the sun disappeared behind some peaks on the island. "Oh Scott, this *is* a wonderful surprise!"

"And if you look out the other window to the southeast you can see Maui's Kahului Bay. We're about two and a half miles offshore. You can barely see it, but straight ahead of us is our submarine dock." Scott pointed to a small white building on the shore. "That's where all our guests board one of our two submarines to come out here."

"But I thought the resort was completely under water."

"Most of it is, except for the sun deck down below and, if you look out the doors, the large wind generators. We use the trade winds here to generate most of the power for this place."

Rebecca peeked out the door windows and saw a maintenance deck to each side, extending the full length of the structure. Above the deck on each side of the vestibule were six round, louvered openings with what seemed to be twelve-foot diameter fans turning inside. When Rebecca looked back out the southeast window, she could see the lights of Kahului shimmering across the bay.

"Do you want to go out on the sun deck?" Scott asked.

"Yes, that would be nice." Rebecca was surprised Scott didn't try to make out with her, as this vestibule would have been the perfect place to do it.

They climbed back down the stairs to the elevator lobby and stepped outside onto the sun deck. Even with the sun going down, Rebecca felt the heat and humidity of the tropical island. She could smell the ocean lapping at the superstructure around them. On the sun deck, she saw some couples embracing and watching the last few moments of the sunset. *This is so romantic!* It would be so cool to be here with her husband on their honeymoon.

Again Scott looked at his watch.

"That's a nice watch, Scott."

"Thanks, my dad gave me this watch. It has a GPS tracker chip in it in case I get kidnapped."

"I guess you can't sneak out either unless you leave your watch behind."

He shook his head. "Rebecca, my dad is about to give his little speech before the show in the main restaurant. You've got to see this show! It's like totally awesome!"

"Okay, I'll take your word for it. So far, the tour has been great. Lead the way."

They went back into the elevator and took it down to the next level. Scott took Rebecca's hand again and led her around the atrium opening to a short corridor at one end of the resort. At the end of the corridor was an arched entrance. A young Polynesian woman stood before a counter piled with menus.

"Hi Ani, how are you doing? Has my dad gone on yet?" Scott asked.

"Scotty!" Ani exclaimed with a huge smile as she ran out from behind the desk and gave him a hug. "I'm doing fine. It's so good to see you again. Your father is just about to go on. You want I get you a table?"

"No, we can just stand somewhere out of the way. This is my new friend Rebecca. She has never been here before."

Ani smiled at Rebecca. "Okay Scotty, you come with me. Ani has just the place for you."

Rebecca wondered how Scott knew this girl so well.

Ani led them around the bamboo partition behind the counter and up onto the platform on the other side, where the sound engineer sat. She got two stools for them to sit on. From there, Rebecca could see all around the restaurant. Along the outside walls were large curved glass panels. Tables followed the windows all around the room. Below their perch was a small stage with a microphone and a man sitting at a keyboard playing easy-listening mood music. Mr. Anderson walked up on the stage to the microphone.

"Ladies and gentlemen, welcome to Lalokai Resort. I'm Ashley Anderson, the owner. I'm so glad you've chosen to stay with us. We hope you enjoy your visit here, and if you have any problems during your stay, please let us know. We're here to serve you, and now on with the show!"

As Mr. Anderson left the stage, the sound technician in front of them dimmed the house lights and brought up flood lights outside the windows. Then the room filled with recorded music and a wall of bubbles rose in front of the windows. When the bubbles cleared, Rebecca could see beautiful women in mermaid costumes swimming outside all around them. For the next fifteen minutes, they put on an undersea ballet in time with the music. They each gave a little bow at the end of the show as the sound technician announced their names. All the guests applauded as the bubble curtain outside returned and the mermaids disappeared.

"So what did you think of the show?" Scott asked.

"Totally awesome! It was beautiful. The skill of the performers was incredible. How are they able to breathe for so long under water?"

"They have special gear as part of their costumes. If there's time, I'll take you downstairs to their locker room, but first, I want to show you one of the luxury suites."

They returned to the elevator and went down one level to the main lobby. Scott took Rebecca around the atrium opening to the submarine landing, where she saw staff unloading supplies.

"Unlike other hotels, our lobby is near the top of the structure. All the rooms are on the lower levels with the best suites on the bottom by the ocean floor." They walked around the atrium opening to the front desk.

Nearby, there was a model of the resort in a glass case. Rebecca studied the model to get a better idea of what the place looked like on the outside. It truly was an incredible piece of engineering.

"Hi, Leilani! I see you're still working the front desk. Are there any empty suites?" Scott asked the young Polynesian woman. "I want my friend Rebecca to see what they look like."

"Scotty, you're back!" Leilani squealed with delight as she ran from behind the desk and threw her arms around him. "How are you doing? You're all grown up into such a big handsome young man." Leilani felt his arm muscles.

"I'm doing alright. Can you please see if there are any suites not being used?"

"Sure Scotty, whatever the owner's son wants, Leilani will give him," she said with a wink. "Yes, we have some suites open. Here,

I'll give you the key for Room 107 so you and your girlfriend can be alone." Leilani gave Scott a wry smile.

"No, *you* don't understand, Leilani; I'm not that kind of guy. I just need someone from housekeeping to open the room and stay around so Rebecca can see what it looks like inside. Nothing more."

"I'm sorry, Scotty. I'll take a break and show you the room myself. Kalei, you have the front desk! I'm going on break," she called out to a woman in the back room.

They followed Leilani to the elevator and took it down to the bottom floor where she led them to Room 107 and opened the door for them.

"Please leave the door open," Scott asked as he and Rebecca entered the suite.

Leilani stood at the doorway while Scott and Rebecca surveyed the suite. As suites went, it was small—more like a cabin on a cruise ship. Rebecca saw two large windows, a king size bed, a small table and chairs, and a private bathroom. Scott walked over to the windows and pushed a button, which turned on some flood lights outside. Rebecca could see the ocean floor with all the colorful coral, fish and sea creatures. It was like having your own private saltwater aquarium.

"This is like so cool Scott. I can see why people want to stay here," Rebecca remarked.

"Yes, this place is unique. Our guests have to book some of these rooms a year in advance. We get lots of couples on their honeymoon. It's nine o'clock Rebecca. We'd better get going."

"Thank you, Leilani," Rebecca said as she left the suite.

"You're welcome. Scotty, please don't tell your father I did this for you," she pleaded.

"You have nothing to fear, Leilani. Thank you for showing us the suite."

Leilani returned to the front desk, and Scott took Rebecca to the end of the corridor below the restaurant. Again, he used his badge to gain access to the mermaid's locker room. Scott walked up to a door at the end of the room, cracked it open, and yelled, "Is anyone in here? Is it okay for us to come in?"

"Come on in, we've changed into our clothes," came a voice from inside the dressing room.

Scott and Rebecca walked into the room past the lockers and showers to the airlock at the end of the room, where a light was on. Inside, they saw two drop-dead gorgeous women sitting on stools next to one of the couches where the performers donned their mermaid costumes. They had some access panels open on the costume tail, exposing the equipment inside.

"Hi, Sophie!" Scott said. "I was hoping you were still here. This is my friend Rebecca. She wanted to see your costumes more closely."

"Scotty! It's so good to see you again," the dark-haired, blue-eyed young woman exclaimed as she put down her tools and embraced him. "The last time I saw you was a couple of years ago. How are you doing?"

"I'm doing fine. I still work for my dad wherever he needs me. I'm almost eighteen and will be going to college next year. I'm not sure yet which college I'll attend. Probably someplace with a good engineering and business school. I see you're still doing the show."

"Yes, but that's only a small part of my responsibilities. Your father has put me in charge of filling the air tanks with Nitrox and maintaining the costumes since I designed them. I'm using my degree in robotics from MIT to keep fake mermaid tails operational. This is Cheryl. I'm training her to assist me so that I can be free to take some time off."

A lady next to her with long, blond hair and blue eyes waved to them.

"Can you explain to Rebecca how your costumes work?"

"I'd be happy to." Sophie opened another access panel. For the next few minutes, Sophie showed Rebecca all the intricacies of the mermaid costumes.

"Cool!" Rebecca exclaimed. "Thanks, Sophie for showing me how everything works on your costumes." She wondered if Scott was just another rich playboy. How did he know all these beautiful women?

"Yes, thanks, Sophie," Scott said. "We'd better head back, Rebecca. It's almost ten o'clock."

"Goodbye Scotty and Rebecca, don't be strangers. You're welcome to visit anytime," Sophie said.

Scott took Rebecca's hand and led her back out of the locker room and down the corridor, past all the suites to the atrium again. They got into the elevator and took it up to the fourth floor.

"I'm afraid this concludes our tour of the Lalokai Resort, me lady." Scott spoke with a stuffy British accent again. "I'm sorry we didn't have time to see the shopping area and the recreational facilities. They're all in the wing on the other side of the atrium from the restaurant."

"That's okay, Scott. I still had a wonderful time with you and really enjoyed the tour. Can I ask you some personal questions?"

"Certainly, you can always ask, but that doesn't mean I'll answer them," Scott teased.

"How is it that you know all these ladies here at the resort?"

"When I was thirteen my dad had me start working as an assistant to the maintenance personnel. It's part of his plan to groom me for taking over as CEO someday. So I ran all over the resort helping them fix things and maintain the place. I still have my access badge as you can see, because I help out here when I can. Needless to say, I got to know all the staff here at the resort. Those ladies haven't seen me for two years, so I guess they were just glad to have me back again. You're not jealous, are you?"

"Oh no, I was just curious," Rebecca said with a coy smile. "What did you mean when you said earlier that, your 'true home is not of this world?'"

"That's just my way of saying that because everyone in my family are Christians, we are no longer part of this world, but citizens of Heaven. When we accepted Jesus Christ as our Savior and Lord, we became part of God's family. So now our real home is in Heaven because we have a relationship with the only true and living God, through Jesus Christ."

"I never knew rich people were so religious. I always thought they're just a bunch of spoiled, greedy, power-hungry snobs."

"It's true that some wealthy people abuse their privileges. Some of them are the most miserable people I've ever met. But we believe prosperity has responsibilities and is in some ways more dangerous than poverty. Most of the rich people I know worked very hard to obtain their success. And real Christianity is more about a relationship with God than a bunch of religious rituals."

"I'm glad to know you guys aren't stuck-up. You folks seem very nice. Of course, I haven't met very many rich people."

"Oh, so you prefer to believe a stereotype?"

"I guess I'll have to revise my opinion of the wealthy. You've given me some food for thought, Scott. Are you always this pushy?"

"What do you mean?"

"All evening it's been go, go, go. Don't get me wrong; I enjoyed seeing the resort. I just think we could have gone at a more leisurely pace."

"I'm sorry, Rebecca. I thought I was just a good host. I didn't want you to miss anything."

"That may be so, but you could have been a little less intense about it. Would it be the end of the world if we didn't get back by ten o'clock?"

Disappointment covered Scott's face, and he just shut up. He looked like a puppy that had just been scolded for wetting the floor. Once again, they straddled one of the scooters to return to the research facility. Rebecca followed Scott back to his family's living quarters, and they all turned in for the night.

As Rebecca lay in the cozy bed, she pondered everything that had happened that day. *I'm such an idiot!* Why did I scold Scott? He'd looked so hurt; *great way to treat a guy who only wanted to show you the resort, Rebecca. Of course, he did deserve it. Scott is a really nice guy, but he's so religious. And he sure doesn't know how to relate to me. Still it would be cool to have a rich boyfriend.* Even if he wasn't rich, Scott was way better than any guy she had ever met, but Rebecca wasn't sure how he felt about her. Maybe he was just being nice and wasn't really interested in her. At least he didn't try to hook up with her, like Butch. He'd certainly had plenty of opportunities! Rebecca earnestly hoped that Scott would want her for his girlfriend because he clearly knew how to respect her. *No wonder all those women at the resort like him so much! Oh, but what if he already has a girlfriend?* Rebecca decided she had to get to know Scott better in hope that he would choose her for his girlfriend. But what could she do to get his attention?

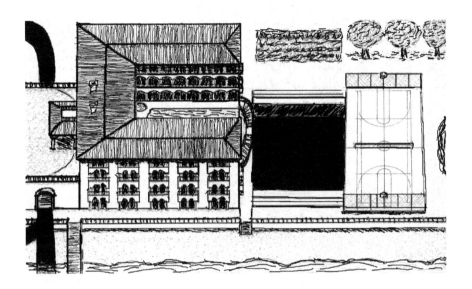

CHAPTER 5

The Journey Home

The next morning, Rebecca awoke to the sound of someone knocking on the door. "Rebecca dear, you need to get up now. We have a long journey ahead of us today," Mrs. Anderson said.

"What time is it?" Rebecca groaned.

"It's six o'clock, dear. Breakfast will be ready soon."

Rebecca quickly took a shower and got dressed. When she came into the dining room, Scott and his parents were already sitting at the table, eating. She sat down and began dishing up scrambled eggs and pancakes from the platters on the table.

"Do you guys always get up this early in the morning?" Rebecca asked.

"Yes, we normally get up early," Mr. Anderson said. "We need to leave right after breakfast."

When they finished eating, Rebecca brushed her teeth and joined them in the living room. Mr. and Mrs. Anderson and Scott bid her to join hands with them as Mr. Anderson prayed for God to grant them a safe trip back to Whatcom.

Then the Andersons picked up their small overnight bags, and they all got into the elevator to go down to the floor below. Mr. and Mrs. Anderson walked down the hall hand-in-hand with Scott and Rebecca following close behind them. They went into a small dressing room with benches and lockers. Rebecca noticed that the flight suits had been removed from the aircraft and then placed in the dressing room. A couple of staff members came in to assist them into their flight suits. Rebecca also saw that someone had put her name on a suit, which she thought was very considerate.

Once they were suited up, Mr. Anderson led them through a door and down the ramp to the aircraft. They each climbed down the ladder into the flight compartment. After stowing their bags in one of the lockers, Mr. Anderson strapped into the pilot's seat and began powering up the aircraft. Mrs. Anderson sat behind her husband, and Rebecca sat behind Scott's seat. After the techs had pulled up the ladder, Scott closed the hatch above them. Scott took his seat, then he and his dad went through their preflight check list.

Rebecca saw red flashing lights on the hanger ceiling and heard Mike in the control room tell all personnel to clear the hanger. Water flooded the hanger with a loud whoosh. When the water reached the ceiling, the hanger doors opened. Scott powered up the water jets, and Mr. Anderson eased the aircraft forward after Mike released the clamps on the pylons. Once they cleared the hanger, Scott pulled back on the throttle lever, and they sped off into the aqua colored water.

After about twenty minutes, Mr. Anderson steered the aircraft towards the surface as Scott began purging the ballast tanks of water. Scott pulled all the way back the aqua jet throttle lever, and they sprang up out of the water, nose first.

"Hang on everyone! It could be a bit bumpy until we get airborne," Mr. Anderson said.

The aircraft skimmed just above the ocean's surface. Scott opened the doors to the jet engine intake and exhaust and began firing them up. The aircraft followed each dip and crest of the waves, like a roller coaster might. Rebecca heard the roar of the dual jet engines behind them and could feel the aircraft lifting up off the water as Mr. Anderson gently pulled back on the stick between his legs and the engine throttle levers at the same time. Scott set their course on the navigation computer and shut down and retracted the aqua jets. Now they were flying about 100 feet off the water's surface.

"Okay everyone, here we go," Mr. Anderson said through their radios. He pulled back on the stick, causing the aircraft to shoot up into the air. When they reached the proper elevation, he leveled off the aircraft and banked it towards the northeast. Rebecca felt her body press back into the seat as they ascended, and her ears popped. She felt as heavy as though she'd gained two hundred pounds!

"It's time for some traveling music, Scott," Mr. Anderson said.

"Ashley dear, I think Rebecca should choose what we listen to since she is our guest," Mrs. Anderson suggested. "What kinds of music do you like, Rebecca?"

"I like country and pop music, but you can listen to whatever you want," Rebecca said.

"No, we want you to enjoy your time with us. Who are your favorite artists?"

"I like Alan Jackson."

"You hear that, Scott? See what we have in the database," Mrs. Anderson said.

"Yes, Mom, cueing up Alan Jackson now."

"Mr. Anderson, can I ask you a question?" Rebecca asked.

"Yes, what would you like to know?"

"Do you think there is any chance for me to work as a chef at your resort?"

"We have all the staff we need right now, but you're always welcome to apply for a job. Just go to the resort's website and click on the Employment menu."

"Thank you, sir. I think your resort is like so cool. I hope someday I can work there or at least stay there. I'd love to spend more time in Hawaii! I've never been anywhere outside of Whatcom before this trip, except to visit relatives in Eastern Washington. You folks have been so kind to me. I've enjoyed my visit with you. This has been quite an adventure. One I will never forget. It's too bad I have to go back to my old routine in Whatcom."

"You're welcome, Rebecca," Mr. Anderson said. "I'm sorry if I came off so gruff when we first met. I was upset after all the delays. I've had time to cool off and reflect on things, and I believe God brought you into our lives for a reason. I'm not sure what that is yet, but I know He uses all our circumstances for our own good. My wife and I will be sending an invitation with you when you return home for your entire family to come to our house for a barbecue. We'd like to get to know you folks better. We don't know very many people in Whatcom because my work requires me to do a lot of traveling. I hope you will want to come. We don't bite."

"Really? That'd be like totally awesome!"

For the next couple of hours, Rebecca relaxed and listened to music while Scott and his parents conversed.

"Daniel told me he had to shoot another drone out of the sky over our property today," Mr. Anderson said. "Honestly, I wish these people would leave us alone."

"And then there was the time last week when the guards had to stop those spies from coming onshore from Lake Whatcom late at night," Scott said. "These guys are relentless."

Rebecca hadn't realized the Andersons led such risky lives. She wanted to ask if Scott had a girlfriend but thought better of it. Maybe it wasn't worth it to be his girlfriend if they were always being threatened by spies.

As they approached the Washington coast, Scott shut down the wing rockets and slowed the aircraft to subsonic speed. Within minutes, they descended and approached the foothills of the Cascade Mountains and Whatcom. Mr. Anderson brought them down to 500 feet above Lake Whatcom and banked the aircraft around over their estate while Scott fired the landing rockets. Rebecca caught a glimpse of Bellingham in the distance as they turned. A Mediterranean-style villa in the shape of a U, with a courtyard and pool in the middle, came into view. She saw the tennis and basketball court roll back, exposing a large rectangular hole in the back yard, and then heard the landing gear come down with a thump. Mr. Anderson shut down the two jet engines and hovered over the hole. He carefully descended, watching the screen on his instrument panel the whole time, to align the aircraft with the opening.

When they were only twenty-five feet above the ground, Rebecca got a better view of the villa, but only for a few seconds. It had a red tile roof, beige stucco walls, and black wrought iron handrails around the courtyard. Darkness swallowed them up as they dropped down into the opening in the ground. Smoke filled the space as Mr. Anderson landed. After the smoke had cleared, the covering rolled back into place, and Mr. Anderson shut down the aircraft. Immediately, two maintainers approached the aircraft to begin hooking up hoses and placing chocks by the wheels. They got out of their seats and Scott opened the hatch on the floor while Mrs. Anderson assisted Rebecca out of her flight suit.

As they climbed down the ladder into the hanger, Rebecca smelled the lingering odor of smoke. She followed the Andersons past shelves filled with boxes of spare parts and into the basement under the house.

"Is it alright if I show Rebecca our house?" Scott asked.

"Yes dear, but lunch will be ready soon, so don't take too long," Mrs. Anderson said.

"Do you want to see our house, Rebecca?" Scott asked.

"Yes, I'd love another tour!"

"Awesome! Let's start down here in the basement." Scott proceeded to show Rebecca all around his family's home. Rebecca was very impressed. When they walked into Scott's bedroom, Rebecca saw a double bed near the doorway, across from a window with a view of Lake Whatcom, and a desk with a laptop on it at the other end, by the window facing the backyard. All around them, on the walls, hung photos of sports cars and airplanes. He also had some model cars and airplanes on shelves. Hanging neatly on one wall were skis, a snowboard, a tennis racket, a baseball bat and glove, and a fencing foil and mask. One thing Rebecca noticed was that there were no photos of girls on his walls—unlike her younger brother

Roger's room. She looked inside the modest bathroom at the other end of the room and saw a walk-in closet next to it. Everything was neat and orderly, again, unlike Roger's room. She partly closed the door to see what was behind it and found a painting of the house hanging on the wall.

"Did you paint this picture?"

"Yes, it's not very good, but my parents insisted I try painting and all sorts of things as part of my education."

"Actually Scott, your painting isn't that bad. I assume you painted this house, right?"

"Yes, it was kind of fun, but I don't see myself becoming a famous artist."

"Your room is very nice, Scott. I can actually see the floor. My brother's room looks like a landfill!"

"Thanks, Rebecca. I like to have everything in place and a place for everything. Besides, my mom would kill me if I didn't keep my room clean."

Scott pulled a gospel tract from his desk and handed it and his phone to Rebecca. "Rebecca, here's my contact information and something I'd like you to read and think about. If you don't mind, I'd also like your address and phone number. I want to stay in touch with you. I don't have many friends in Whatcom since I don't go to school here, and I really want to be your friend."

Oh no, not the friend zone! "No problem Scott." She smiled as she put her contact information in his phone and his in her phone. She placed the tract and her phone in her jeans pocket after handing his phone back. *What's this guy's problem? Why isn't he asking me out? Maybe he's just too shy to ask. He is a little awkward around me.*

The intercom by the door crackled to life and Mrs. Anderson said, "Lunch is ready. We're eating in the kitchen."

Scott pushed the button and replied, "We'll be right down, Mom."

They walked down the corridor by the courtyard, to the elevator in the middle of the house, which was located next to two curved stairways leading down to the foyer. Mrs. Anderson was just placing a plate of sandwiches and some soup on the table at one end of the large kitchen when they entered. Scott and Rebecca sat at the table with Mrs. Anderson, and Scott gave thanks for the food.

"I'm afraid Ashley won't be joining us for lunch," Mrs. Anderson said. "He's meeting with the staff. Here, Rebecca, I'd like you to give this to your parents when you get home." She handed an envelope to her.

"What kind of sandwiches are these? They're delicious," Rebecca asked.

"They're called Monte Cristo sandwiches, dear."

"You have a beautiful home, Mrs. Anderson."

"Thanks, it suits our needs. Now when you've finished your lunch, dear, I'll tell Daniel to bring the car around so we can get you back to your family."

"Can I go with them, Mom?" Scott asked. "I'd like to see where Rebecca lives."

"Yes Scott, you may go too." After lunch, Mrs. Anderson pushed the button on the intercom for Daniel's quarters. "Daniel, please bring the car around. We have a young lady to take home."

"Sure thing Mrs. A, I'll be right out," Daniel said.

After Scott and Rebecca had helped Mrs. Anderson clear the table, they walked out to the foyer and through the large, carved front doors. A white Rolls-Royce was waiting for them, and a large, middle-aged black man in a dark suit stood by the rear door. As they approached, the man opened the car door.

"Hi Daniel, this is Rebecca. Here's her address in Whatcom." Scott handed a sticky-note to him.

"Hey Mr. Scott, Miss Rebecca," Daniel greeted them as they entered the car.

"Daniel is not only our driver and mechanic, but he's also our head of security, my mixed martial arts instructor, and my basketball coach," Scott said as they drove around the circular driveway and out towards the main gate. "He used to be a Navy SEAL."

CHAPTER 6

The Turning Point

The white Rolls-Royce carried them down the lane from the Anderson's estate to the outskirts of Whatcom.

"I don't want to alarm you Mr. Scott, but there's a black SUV following us from a distance," Daniel said.

"Thanks, Daniel. I'm sure you know what to do if they get too close," Scott said. "Don't worry Rebecca; this car is built like a tank."

"That's a relief! Riding in this car makes me feel like a princess. This is so cool," Rebecca said.

"You deserve to be treated like a princess," Scott said. "You really are something special. You're not only beautiful but are intelligent and have a generous spirit. God loves you so much, more than you can imagine."

"Well, I think *you* are pretty special. If I'm a princess, then you must be a prince! I've never met a guy like you, Scott."

"Oh, I'm not perfect Rebecca, but I do try to be a gentleman."

"You seem pretty perfect to me! The guys I have to deal with at school can't hold a candle to you! They're all a bunch of immature jerks. But you know how to treat a girl with respect."

Scott turned his head away. As they reached downtown Whatcom, Daniel turned onto the main street through town. Downtown Whatcom was typical for a small town in America, with its brick facades and large picture windows for each business. All of the businesses sported some kind of neon signage to beckon customers inside. The gaudiest of these was the Bijou Theater's sign. Rebecca watched as everyone along the street turned to gawk at them.

"Oh, look! There's my dad's sporting goods store. And there's Rick's Diner; they have like the best burgers in town! Everybody hangs out at Rick's." Rebecca saw a bemused smirk on Scott's face. "What's so funny?"

"Oh, I just think you're cute when you get so excited. You're acting like a cheerleader with two shots of espresso in her system. I've never seen you so animated."

"That's because I *am* a cheerleader. There's my high school. Go Wolverines!"

Daniel turned the corner onto her street. The black SUV was no longer in sight. He brought the car to a stop in front of an older, white, two-story house with a white picket fence, blue shutters and trim, and a porch that wrapped around the front—complete with a bench swing. Rebecca reached to open the door, but Scott stopped her.

"Please let Daniel do it, Princess."

"Well, I guess it's time to face the music." Rebecca leaned over and kissed him on the cheek. "It was nice meeting you, Scott. I really enjoyed spending time with you and your family."

"We enjoyed having you as a stowaway. I'll check later to see how you're doing. Hopefully, your parents won't keep you in solitary confinement too long," Scott teased as Daniel opened the car door.

Both Rebecca and Scott got out of the car. He waited by the car as she scampered up the walkway. She turned and waved to them from the porch as he got back into the car next to Daniel, and then they drove away.

When Rebecca came through the front door, she saw her dad in the living room watching TV and heard her Mom in the kitchen fussing with dinner. *Roger must be upstairs in his room.* "Hey everybody, I'm home!"

Elaine Robinson came running from the kitchen and grabbed Rebecca with a huge hug. Her father soon followed.

"Oh honey, we were so worried about you; don't ever do that to us again!" Mrs. Robinson cried.

"I'm sorry, Mom and Dad. I never meant to hurt you. Oh, Mrs. Anderson gave this to me, for you." Rebecca handed the envelope to her dad.

He opened it and read it aloud:

"Dear Mr. and Mrs. Robinson:

We hope that you won't be too hard on Rebecca. We've forgiven her and found her to be a fine young lady. We'd like to get to know you all better, and wish to extend an invitation to you all to come to our home for a barbecue as soon as both our schedules allow. R.S.V.P. Enclosed is a map to our place and our phone number. Please give me a call.

Mary Ann Anderson"

"Can we go, Daddy? Please, Daddy, they're awfully nice people."

"Yes, I suppose we could see how the other half lives; does that handsome boy I saw you get out of their car with have anything to do with your eagerness for a visit?" Mr. Robinson teased.

"Dad! His name is Scott. He's their only child and yes, I'm crushing on him big time. Unlike the boys at school, Scott's a perfect gentleman."

"Then I guess we better call the Andersons. Meanwhile, your mother and I have come to a decision. From now on, you're not to go anywhere alone. As for your punishment, you will be cleaning the house by yourself for the next month."

"Okay, Daddy. Can I go to my room now? I'm really tired and could use a nap before supper." Inside, though, Rebecca resolved not to comply with their wishes. *I'm almost an adult and can go anywhere I want. Who are they to tell me where I can and cannot go?*

As Rebecca walked down the hall to her room, she heard her brother Roger call out, "What happened to you, Sis? Why'd you have to come back?"

"I love you too, you brat! I'll tell everyone about my grand adventure at supper."

Rebecca slept for the rest of the afternoon. Finally, her mother came into her room and woke her up for supper. She shared everything that happened with her family at the dinner table that evening.

"Man, you get all the breaks Sis; does Scott have a sister? I'd love to have a rich girlfriend," Roger said.

"Sorry Roger, Scott's an only child," Rebecca replied. "And even if he did have a fourteen-year-old sister, what makes you think she would want to have anything to do with you?"

"I was hoping you wouldn't come back so I could have your room."

"Roger!" His parents yelled in unison.

"Hey, I'm just trying to be realistic."

"I think you need to go to *your* room young man until you can show more compassion towards your sister," Mr. Robinson barked.

Roger slinked up the stairs to his room. Rebecca helped her Mom with the dirty dishes. Afterward, she went to her room to finish her homework. Before she went to bed, Rebecca texted her best friend Loretta to tell her all the details of what had happened. During their conversation, she let it slip that Scott was a hunk and a perfect gentleman.

"Shut up! You mean to tell me you finally found a guy you like? I hope everything works out. So has Scott like called you back yet? When can I meet your Prince Charming?"

"It hasn't even been one day yet! Besides, I don't know if he's interested in me, other than being friends. So, are you like ready for the calculus quiz Monday?"

"Are you kidding? Calculus and I don't get along at all! Oh, I've decided to try and get Butch to go out with me."

"I still think you're making a big mistake Loretta, but I want you to be happy. I'd better let you go. I'm still exhausted after traveling so much this weekend."

"I'm so glad you're back Rebecca. I was like so scared I'd never see you again."

Scott waited for a couple of days before video chatting with Rebecca. "Hey Rebecca, how are you doing? Do I need to send a cake with a file in it?"

"Hi Scott, I'm doing okay. I think I got off easy. I only have to clean the house for a month. Your mom will be getting a call from my mom. It looks like we're coming for a visit."

"Great! I look forward to meeting your family."

"Listen, I read that pamphlet you gave me, and I've got some questions. I'm not sure why you gave it to me. We go to church most Sundays at St. Paul's, and it's not like I've ever done anything bad. Believe it or not, I'm a good Christian girl. So why did you give me the pamphlet?"

"Rebecca, do you want to go to Heaven when you die?"

"Of course, I do. Doesn't everybody?"

"And if you were standing at the pearly gates what would you say if God asked you, 'Why should I let you into My Heaven?'"

"I would say because I have done more good things than bad."

"Rebecca, do you believe the Bible is God's Word to us and the absolute truth?"

"I don't think there is such a thing as absolute truth. The Bible is open to interpretation in so many ways; how can you even know it's reliable?"

Rebecca was starting to get uncomfortable with the direction the conversation was going.

"By your own statement, you have contradicted yourself; for to say there is no such thing as absolute truth is to assert an absolute truth in itself. Also, I think you would agree that the laws of physics are pretty absolute—especially gravity. If I jump off a cliff, there's an absolute certainty that I'll plunge to my death unless I do something to counteract the force of gravity. Hence, there *is* absolute truth in the universe."

"Okay, smarty, I can see that, so what?"

"So as for the Bible, its accuracy is more reliable than the works of Plato regarding the ancient manuscripts available to document its content. There's more evidence to support the veracity of the Bible than all of that ancient Greek philosopher's writings. Therefore, the translations we have today are completely reliable. All the textual differences are very minor."

"Alright, you got me there, professor. What's your point?"

"Given what I just said, do you think it's possible that the Bible is God's way of speaking to us today?"

"I guess so. But isn't the Bible full of contradictions and myths?"

"If you believe that the Bible is God's word to us today, then it follows that He'd only tell us the truth and certainly wouldn't contradict Himself. God is most holy and cannot lie. Therefore, can you accept that the Bible is true, Rebecca?"

"Yes, I accept that the Bible is true. I don't understand most of it, but I will concede that it's true. I need to go to bed Scott. I'm glad you called. Why don't you come over tomorrow after school and we can continue this discussion? And if you're good, I might even make you some supper." Rebecca thought that would be a good way to get Scott to visit her.

"Okay, good night. I'll see you tomorrow afternoon."

When Scott arrived at the door of the Robinson home the next day, Rebecca came outside, and they sat on the porch swing. Rebecca sat at one end and Scott at the other. He placed his Bible in between them. Rebecca was annoyed because she was hoping he would sit right next to her.

"Now, as you recall from last night, we established that the Bible is true." Scott picked up his Bible and opened it.

"Yes, yes, so what if the Bible is true? What does that have to do with anything?"

"Then we all have a problem, Rebecca because God tells us in Romans, chapter three, verses ten and eleven, 'As it is written, There is none righteous, no, not one; There is none who understands; There is none who seeks after God . . . .' and in verse twenty-three it says, 'for all have sinned and fall short of the glory of God.' Also Titus, chapter three, verse five says, 'not by works of righteousness which we have done, but according to His mercy He saved us, by the washing of regeneration and renewing of the Holy Spirit . . . .' What this means Rebecca is that we can *never* do enough good deeds to earn our way into Heaven, and what's worse, we all come short of God's holy standard. It's like trying to jump the Grand Canyon. No matter how far you can jump, it's never far enough."

Rebecca began to squirm a little on the swing. "Then how can anyone hope ever to get to Heaven?"

"That's the dilemma. On the one hand, God is infinitely Holy and must punish sin, but on the other hand, He wants to have a relationship with us. Therefore, He loves us so much He sent His sinless Son, Jesus Christ, to take the rap for us. The Bible says in Romans chapter five, verse eight, 'But God demonstrates His own love towards us, in that while we were still sinners, Christ died for us.' And I'm sure you've heard of John three, sixteen, but here it is with a twist: 'For God so loved Rebecca that He gave His only begotten Son, that if she believes in Him, she should not perish but have everlasting life.' In Romans six, verse twenty-three it says, 'For the wages of sin is death, but the gift of God is eternal life in Christ Jesus our Lord.' Our rightful paycheck for our sins is death, but God gave us a wonderful gift through Jesus Christ. But like any gift, you can't have it unless you accept it. So, to go to Heaven, we must accept Jesus Christ as our own personal Savior. We must let Him take our punishment for our sins through faith in Him."

"Alright preacher, just how do I do that? What must I do to accept this gift?"

"Rebecca, if you believe with all your heart that Jesus, as the sinless God-Man, died on the cross, was buried, rose physically from the grave, and is alive today for *you*; you'll be saved. It's that simple. Tell Jesus in prayer that you want Him to be your Savior."

Rebecca's heart pounded, and she could hear the blood throbbing in her ears. She sensed a terrible weight pressing upon her. She bowed her head to pray. "Jesus, this is Rebecca. I want you to be my Savior. I do believe that when you died on the cross, you did it for me. Please help me, Amen."

"If you sincerely meant that Rebecca, then welcome to the family of God! Because everyone who receives Jesus as their Savior has the authority to be part of God's family. God adopts us. How cool is that?"

"That's wonderful! I can't explain it, but I feel somehow different Scott. It's like having complete peace of mind or an inner calm I never had before. Freaky!"

"That's the peace of God; it goes with the territory when you accept Christ. You have the Holy Spirit living inside you. Now that you're born again into God's family, you need spiritual food. You should read the Bible daily. I suggest you start with the Gospel of John and then continue to the rest of the New Testament instead of starting at the beginning as you might with any other book. You also should talk to God every day through prayer. Just take your problems to Him, thank Him, and praise Him. You should pray for others, too."

"Thank you, Scott. I don't own a Bible, but I'm sure we must have one somewhere around here."

"Well, we'll have to do something about that. I feel I should warn you—since you're now part of God's family, the devil may come after you with a vengeance. So don't be surprised if you have more problems than usual in the next few days. But I'll be praying for you and your protection from Satan and his demons. I'm so happy for you, Rebecca."

"Thanks, Scott. There's so much I don't know about this stuff! Now, how about I fix us something to eat? Wait here; I'll be right back."

Rebecca disappeared into the house for a few minutes and came back carrying a tray with some sandwiches and sodas on it, which she placed in the middle of the bench swing. Scott took her hand out of habit and gave thanks to God for the food and for saving Rebecca. Rebecca was so thrilled to have Scott hold her hand she almost forgot to eat her sandwich. Scott quietly ate his sandwich. While they were eating, an old black Chevy pickup drove by with Butch and his buddies in it. Butch glared at Rebecca.

"Oh no, it's Butch! Now I'll never hear the end of it at school."

"Who's Butch? Is he your boyfriend?"

"Now who's jealous?" she teased. "Butch is Sheriff Brown's son. He has this mistaken notion that I should be his girlfriend, but I want nothing to do with him!"

"If he gives you any trouble, just let me know. I'll be happy to educate him."

"Thanks, Scott, that means a lot to me."

"I'd better get home, Princess. We both have school tomorrow."

"Okay, goodbye Scott." Rebecca kissed him on the cheek.

Scott seemed uneasy and just got up, waved, and left. Rebecca was puzzled. How could he be so articulate about the Bible and so awkward around her?

Rebecca received a package the next day with a Bible in it. The Bible had a white cover, and her name embossed on it in gold and came with the following card:

Hey Princess:

Here's a new Bible for you. Now you can get regular meals and 'milk' (1 Peter 2:1-3). May you continue to grow in God's grace. See you soon.

In Christ's love:

Scott

Rebecca sent Scott a text message right away to thank him for the Bible.

On Saturday, Scott called Rebecca to video chat. "Hey Rebecca, how are you doing? Texting is okay, but I wanted to see you and hear your voice."

"Oh hi, Scott; it's good to see you too. Thanks again for the Bible. It was really sweet of you. You even put my name on it! I'll treasure it forever! It's been a hard week. I strained my ankle during cheer practice and then yesterday my science experiment spilled all over. Still, after asking Jesus to be my Savior, I have this inner joy I never had before. I'm worried, though, that my friends won't like me anymore when they find out about my new faith."

"I'm sorry things have been hard for you. I hope you're feeling better soon. I pray for you daily. So—how are you doing with your Bible reading? Have you gotten very far in the Gospel of John?"

"Just having you call has made me feel much better. I just started reading my Bible today, so I'm only through chapter three. My mom told me she talked with your mother. I guess we're coming to your place next Saturday. I can't wait!"

"Me too. Will you go swimming with us?"

"Yes, but I'm not sure about the rest of my family. If I know Roger, he'll be camped at the table eating or playing with your video games. He's always playing some war game."

"Then he'll be disappointed because we don't have any violent video games. We have some sports games and simulators, however. Does Roger like other games? We have a basketball court, foosball, a pool table, and some board games."

"Roger isn't into sports unless it's a video game. My mom says you're serving moose burgers. Now, that's something I've never tasted! How in the world did you ever get moose meat?"

"My father and I like to go hunting and fishing in Alaska. Last summer he shot a moose, and we had it butchered in Anchorage.

We also caught some salmon and brought it all back here to put in our freezer. We've been eating that moose for a long time! Let me ask you something. What do you like to do for fun?"

"Why do you want to know?" Rebecca asked coyly.

"As your friend, I want to know more about you."

"I like hanging out with friends at Rick's Diner. And I like reading, listening to music and, of course, cooking. What about you?"

"Oh, I think you know I like most sports. I play tennis with my mom and dad and play basketball with by best friend Sean, and with Daniel when he's not too busy. I also like flying and driving my Porsche. And now, I better let you go so I can get some sleep *before* and not *during* church tomorrow."

"Okay, good night, Scott. Thanks again for the Bible."

The next week couldn't end soon enough for Rebecca. Despite her concern over the threats to his family, she wanted desperately to see Scott again. She didn't understand, however, why he hadn't asked her out on a date yet. He seemed interested in her enough to be friends. Why not take it to the next level? Rebecca consoled herself with the thought that if they were meant to get together, everything would work out. Maybe God had brought Scott into her life for this purpose. Perhaps Scott would ask her out at the barbecue?

CHAPTER 7

The Flirt

Monday, Loretta sat down next to Butch in the lunchroom at school. He and his buddies were at a table by themselves talking sports and bugging each other. She wanted to get his attention.

"Hey Butch, whatcha doing?" Loretta asked.

"What do you want, Red? Nobody invited you to sit here," Butch said.

"Oh, I just thought maybe you could use some female companionship now that it looks like Rebecca has a new guy in her life."

"What do you mean? Is it that guy I saw her with on her porch the other day? Who is he?"

"His name is Scott, and he's loaded. His family owns Anderson Aerospace."

"That must have been his blue Porsche I saw parked in front of Rebecca's house. Well, he better leave her alone, or I'll show him who's boss around here."

"Oh, are you going to introduce him to your father?"

"Very funny Red, no, I'm going to beat him up and mess up his fancy car."

"I'd pay money to see that, especially if *he* beat you up!"

"Well, why don't you just scram, you pest?" Butch shoved Loretta off the bench and onto the floor.

Loretta promptly picked herself up off the floor and dumped the rest of her smoothie over Butch's head.

"Why you little . . . I'll get you for this!" Butch yelled as he chased her out of the lunchroom. Loretta ran down the hall and ducked into the girls' locker room.

Cracking the door, Butch yelled inside, "You can't hide in there forever, Red!"

Loretta came near the door and cried, "And you can't stand there forever! You hurt me, Butch. I was only trying to be friendly. Can't you see that I like you?"

"Okay, okay, Red. I'm sorry I pushed you on the floor. But you shouldn't have poured your smoothie all over me. Now I'm a sticky mess!"

"I'm sorry too, Butch, but you made me so mad. Honestly, you can be so frustrating!"

"Alright, truce? Let's get a burger at Rick's after school today."

"That would be a good way to make it up to me, okay, truce for now." Loretta came out of the locker room with a towel and wiped most of the remaining smoothie off of Butch. She playfully took her finger and scooped some of it off his shirt and put it in her mouth. "Mmmm, strawberry banana. You're going to have to work a lot harder than that to get rid of me."

"Maybe I don't want to get rid of you." Butch took some of the smoothie from his shirt and placed it on her nose. "See you later Red. I need to get a shower."

After school, Loretta approached a white art deco building with red and white striped awnings over the large windows and red tile work and stainless steel under them. Rick's Diner hearkened back to the 1950s, but with a fresh coat of paint. It was clean and white inside with lots of stainless steel accents like a vintage car, and still had a jukebox that was now loaded with CDs. Its proximity to the high school made it a favorite haunt of the students. Loretta crossed the black and white tiled floor and found Butch sitting by himself in one of the red vinyl upholstered booths. She sat across from him and ordered a hamburger, fries, and a chocolate shake.

"I got chewed out by Mr. Steele for pushing you on the floor. Do you really like me, Red?" Butch asked, dragging a French fry through the puddle of catsup on his plate.

"Yeah, you're fun to torment," Loretta teased. "But seriously yes, I do like you, Butch. You're handsome and strong. And you're the best athlete the Wolverines have."

"What's the deal with this rich kid and Rebecca? Are they serious?"

"I don't know. He hasn't even asked her out yet. She said her family is going to the Anderson estate for a barbecue this Saturday."

"I know where that is; it's the big place just outside of town by the lake. I'd love to see what's inside there. Hey, you want to go to a movie with me Friday, Red?"

"Sure, but I better meet you at the Bijou. My parents aren't too happy about me dating you."

"What's wrong? Don't they think the sheriff's son is good enough for their daughter?"

"As a matter of fact, yes, they don't think you're good enough for me, but I don't care. I'll date whoever I want. Just let them try and stop me! So it would be better if you don't come to the house to pick me up. After the movie, we could go hang out somewhere, and I'll bring some of my dad's beer."

"Being the daughter of a pub owner has its perks, I see. Okay, you bring the beer, and we can go to the park afterward. Did you see the ballgame the other day? We like totally crushed the Red Raiders."

"Yes, that was a monster home run you hit off their pitcher. He was obviously having a very bad day."

"And what about the double play we pulled off in the ninth inning?"

"It was truly a thing of beauty, Butch. Is there any sport you're not good at?"

"I don't play soccer. I think soccer is for sissies. Football is where it's at; now that's a real man's sport."

"I better get home. I still need to do my homework. Thanks for the hamburger. See you tomorrow, Butch."

"Right, Red, see ya."

Loretta walked home, her heart pounding with excitement. She was brimming with anticipation for Friday and her date with Butch. This was so cool. Finally, Butch was paying attention to her. But how could she sneak out? She could never tell her parents she was going with Butch. *I know. I'll tell them I'm meeting my girlfriends at the Bijou.*

Friday evening Loretta met Butch by the Bijou and stashed her backpack with the beer in his truck before they went into the theater.

"I bought the tickets, Red. You get us some popcorn and sodas."

"Of course Butch; you're such a gentleman."

Butch led them to the well-worn red plush seats near the back of the theater, and they settled in for the show. It wasn't long before Butch put his arm around Loretta and drew her close to him to make out.

"Man, this movie is like so lame. Come here, Red."

"Stop—not now, Butch. I want to watch the movie."

"That's just like you, Red, since it's a chick flick!" Butch grabbed a handful of popcorn to stuff in his mouth. The film progressed, and he got more restless. He started plinking the people a few rows in front with the unpopped kernels of popcorn.

Afterward, he drove them to Lake Whatcom Park, and they sat in his truck in the parking lot. Some other couples were there too.

"Give me some beer, Red," Butch said.

"Why didn't you like the movie?" Loretta handed a bottle of beer to him from her backpack. She pulled one out for herself as well.

"I thought it was lame. Not enough action. But I guess you liked it since it was so romantic."

"Yes, I like rom coms. What's wrong with a little romance? You could learn a thing or two from that movie."

"Are you saying I'm not romantic enough for you? Ain't nobody holding a gun to your head, Red. You can leave anytime."

"But I don't want to leave. I just wish you would share your feelings with me, and show me you care about me."

Loretta yearned for Butch to show her some genuine affection.

"Why is it all you girls want to talk about is a guy's feelings? Maybe I don't have any *feelings*. I think you're pretty, Red, and I love your blue eyes. I guess I like you too. So you want me to get all mushy and buy you flowers and candy? Is that romantic enough for you?"

"That's a good start, Butch. Do you really think I'm pretty?"

"Yes, but you're not as beautiful as Rebecca."

"Thanks, you always know just what a girl wants to hear."

Butch tossed his empty beer bottle out the truck's window and pulled out some cigarettes. He was about to light one up when Loretta said, "Please don't! If you want to make out with me, put those away. My mom told me kissing a smoker is like licking an ashtray, and I believe her. My dad used to smoke, and it was just awful being around him."

"Would it be better if I switched to vaping or smoking pot, Red?"

"No, they're not good for you either."

"Alright Red, I'll wait until after you leave. When did you get so high and mighty?"

"I just don't like smoking or the stench. It's like so unhealthy for you, too. As a jock, you should take better care of your body." Loretta slid across the seat to snuggle up next to him.

"Yes, Mother! Now, come here, Red." Butch began kissing her.

For the next ten minutes, they made out until Butch wanted to go too far.

"Butch, I'm not ready to hook up with you yet. We hardly know each other. I think you'd better take me home."

"Great! I take you to a movie, and you're not going to put out. I thought you liked me."

"I do like you, Butch. I'm just not going to have sex with you yet. Maybe after we know each other better, I'll think about it. Is that all you want, Butch? You just want to have sex with me?"

"No, you're fun to be with most of the time. Plus, you can get beer."

"Oh, so now the truth comes out. You only like me because I can sneak my dad's beer."

"I said you're pretty, but not as pretty as Rebecca."

"Well, I'm glad to know you find me at least a little attractive. Now take me home."

Butch dropped her off a block from her house, and she walked the rest of the way. Loretta had mixed emotions about her date with Butch. She was thrilled to spend time with him, but she was disappointed to be his second choice after Rebecca. Maybe if she did hook up with Butch, he would like her better. At least Butch was giving her some affection. Her own father paid little attention to her, except to yell at her for drinking his beer. It was much worse now that she was a woman and not his little girl anymore. But even when she was younger he hadn't given her much affection. Loretta knew her dad had always wanted a boy and resented her. At least her mom loved her. But she longed for her dad's love, too. So . . . Butch was way better than nothing. Since she couldn't tell her parents about her date, she decided to tell Rebecca. *I just hope she doesn't give me a lecture on how bad Butch is again. Why can't everyone be happy for me?*

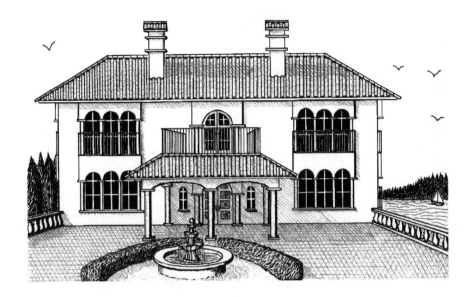

CHAPTER 8

The Barbeque

Saturday morning in mid-April, Rebecca was the first one out of bed. She quickly got ready and packed up her swimsuit and towel in her pink backpack. She helped her Mom finish up the potato salad and baked an apple pie. By ten o'clock they were on their way to the Anderson estate. Mr. Robinson passed through the security gate past the armed guards, went up around the circular driveway, and parked under the porte-cochere by the front door.

When they exited the SUV, the front door opened, and the entire Anderson family emerged to greet them.

"Welcome to Casa di Anderson! I'm Ashley Anderson, and this is my wife Mary Ann and son Scott," Mr. Anderson said as he extended his hand to Mr. Robinson.

"Ralph Robinson, and this is my wife Elaine, son Roger and, of course, daughter Rebecca," he said as he shook Mr. Anderson's hand. "It's so good to meet you finally."

"Please come in, we're eating out in the courtyard." Mr. Anderson led the Robinsons through the foyer to the stairs and down to the recreation room.

"Dude, you have both a racing simulator *and* a flight simulator!" Roger exclaimed as they walked through the room to the courtyard.

"Would you like to try them?" Scott said.

"You bet I would!"

While Scott showed Roger how to use the racing simulator, Mrs. Anderson took the potato salad and apple pie from Mrs. Robinson and Rebecca and placed them on a long table by the barbecue grill, and went back upstairs to the kitchen to get some more food. Mr. Anderson went back to tending the grill after showing his guests where the cold soda was kept. Mr. and Mrs. Robinson sat down in some patio chairs while Rebecca went back into the rec room to find Scott and Roger sitting side by side in the racing simulator cars. Poor Roger was getting "schooled" by Scott on how to drive a race car.

"Dude you're great at this!" Roger said.

"Thanks, I've had plenty of practice here and on a real race track with my dad. As you can see, it takes considerable skill to drive a race car. Hey, Rebecca, you want to try?" Scott asked.

"Okay, but I'm even worse than Roger," she said.

For the next few minutes, Scott let Rebecca sit in his car while he told her how to drive it. They both laughed when she crashed into Roger and then into the wall.

"Well, I reckon I'm ready for driver's education now," Rebecca giggled. "Can we go swimming?"

"Sure, you can change in the bathroom over there," Scott said. "I'll meet you in the pool."

Rebecca emerged from the rec room in her one-piece suit in blue and gold school colors to join Scott in the pool. She admired Scott's well-toned body.

"Come on in the water is warm!"

Rebecca jumped into the shallow end of the pool beside Scott. She felt the tepid water envelope her and gave Scott a playful splash which he returned with gusto.

"Race you to the end of the pool and back," Rebecca said.

"You're on!" Scott said.

Rebecca just barely beat Scott back to the edge of the pool. Scott and Rebecca continued to play in the pool while Mr. and Mrs. Anderson finished up their preparations.

"What do you do for a living Ralph?" Mr. Anderson asked.

"I own Robinson's Sporting Goods in Whatcom. I know it's small potatoes compared to your company, but we're doing alright. We get a lot of business from folks visiting the Cascades or fishing on Lake Whatcom."

"Scott and I will have to check out your store sometime," Mr. Anderson said as he placed the burgers and salmon on platters. "We like to hunt and fish in Alaska, and go fishing on Lake Whatcom, of course. We should get together sometime and go fishing. Okay, everyone, let's eat!"

Scott and Rebecca climbed out of the pool and put on some bathrobes sitting by the pool. Rebecca took off her swim cap allowing her soft blond hair to fall once again upon her shoulders. Mr. Robinson ordered Roger to tear himself away from the simulator and come eat. After everyone had gathered at the patio table, Mr. Anderson clasped his wife's hand and said, "Let's give thanks. Dear Heavenly Father, thank you for this food and for this time to spend with the Robinson family. May we enjoy our fellowship and grow in friendship, in Jesus name, amen."

"Now don't be shy you all, everything is set up buffet style on the table over there. Ralph and Elaine why don't you go first," Mrs. Anderson said.

Everyone helped themselves to the food and returned to the table. Roger quickly wolfed down a moose burger and some potato salad so that he could get back to playing with the racing simulator.

"These moose burgers are delicious Mr. Anderson," Rebecca said. "They're lean and flavorful. Yummy!"

"Thank you, Rebecca. It's always nice to know my cooking is appreciated."

"You folks have a lovely home," Mrs. Robinson said. "Do you live here all the time or do you have other houses too?"

"Elaine this is our primary residence, but we do have living quarters at our resort in Hawaii and a few other places in the world," Mrs. Anderson said. "Ashley has to travel a lot for work. In fact, we're all going to Paris this June for the air show. You folks should come with us. It will give us all a chance to get to know each other better. All you'll need is a valid passport and your luggage. We'll take care of the rest."

"Cool! Oh Dad, can we go. Please?" Rebecca begged.

"It would be nice to take a vacation for a change, Ralph," Mrs. Robinson said.

"Okay, I'll think about it. Are you sure it won't cost us anything? We would be happy to help out with the expenses," Mr. Robinson said.

"Tell us more about going to Paris this summer," Mrs. Robinson asked. "Are you sure it won't be any trouble for us to come with you?"

"No, it won't be any trouble at all," Mrs. Anderson said. "We'll be using our private jet, and we always stay in the penthouse suite at our hotel near Le Bourget airport where the air show's held. There's plenty of room for your family, believe me."

Mrs. Robinson looked at her husband with pleading eyes hoping he would consent to the Anderson's offer. Rebecca knew the look well. Throughout her parents' marriage whenever her mom really wanted something the look was there.

"How long were you planning to be in Paris?" Mr. Robinson asked.

"Since we're going for the air show, one week, but we could stay for two weeks if you wish Ralph," Mr. Anderson said.

"I guess I could leave Bill in charge of the store while we're gone," Mr. Robinson said.

"So we're going?" Mrs. Robinson asked.

"Yes, we accept your offer Ashley," Mr. Robinson said. "We better get some passports right away and start figuring out what to wear."

"Great! I'll take care of the other arrangements. If you wish you can kick in something for any excursions we take," Mr. Anderson said.

"Awesome! Paris this summer! I can hardly wait to tell Loretta! She'll be like so jealous!" Rebecca exclaimed. "Mrs. Anderson you had a chef at the resort I thought for sure you would have one here too."

"Oh, like you Rebecca dear I like cooking. We only employ a chef or caterer here when we have large dinner parties. But when it's just a small group we do the cooking. And as you can see, Ashley likes to barbecue."

"Yes, I find it helps me relax from the stress of work," Mr. Anderson said.

"Could someone show me where the nearest bathroom is?" Mr. Robinson asked.

"I'll show you, Mr. Robinson," Scott said.

After a long time, Mr. Robinson and Scott came out of the rec room and returned to the patio table, where everyone but Roger was enjoying some apple pie with vanilla ice cream. Rebecca handed some to her dad and Scott.

"Mmmmm, this pie is wonderful Mrs. Robinson!" Scott exclaimed.

"Thank you, but Rebecca made it Scott," Mrs. Robinson said. "She's a very good cook. You folks should come to our humble house for dinner sometime."

"We'd enjoy that very much. Just give us a call," Mrs. Anderson said.

"If you will excuse me, I'm going to take a walk around the grounds," Scott said. "Would anyone care to join me?"

Mrs. Robinson started to speak, but her husband took her hand and gave her the "don't" look.

"I'll go with you Scott, just let me change out of my swimsuit first," Rebecca said.

"Oh no, we couldn't let you do that," Scott teased. "We expect all our guests to parade around the grounds in their swim suits."

Rebecca gathered her towel and swim cap, flipped back her long blond hair with a flourish, flung open her bathrobe, and paraded into the rec room like a fashion model. Everyone laughed at her mocking display. Scott collected his sweat clothes and went up to his room to shower and change his clothes. After about ten minutes, he returned wearing blue jeans and a yellow polo shirt. Rebecca sat on the patio in the sun brushing her hair. She was once again wearing blue jeans and a red blouse.

"Are you ready?" Scott asked as he extended his hand toward her.

"Yes, let's go," she said as she stuffed her brush into her backpack and took his hand.

Scott and Rebecca walked past the swimming pool to some steps leading down to the tennis court. Hand in hand they strolled through the tennis court towards the forest and a small pond with two swans and some ducks swimming in it.

As they approached the pond, Rebecca asked Scott, "How big is this estate?"

"We have twenty acres of mostly wooded land here," Scott said. "The property goes all along Lake Whatcom where we have a private beach, boat launch ramp and pier for our boats. We have various fruit and nut trees and a vegetable garden east of the tennis court."

"And your own pond and swans too I see."

"Yeah, my dad used to stock it with fish when I was a little boy. The swans are my mom's idea. I talked to your father today Rebecca, and asked him for permission to court you. He said, 'Yes,' so would you like to go out with me next Friday?"

"Yes!" Rebecca squealed in delight. "I thought you'd never ask. Did you really ask my dad for permission? That's like so old-fashioned and romantic at the same time."

"Yes, he said he would hunt me down like a moose if I hurt you. We could go to Rick's Diner Friday and hang out with your friends."

"Oh, that would be awesome! My BFF Loretta is just dying to meet you." Rebecca turned towards Scott face to face. She placed her arms around his neck and planted a kiss on his lips. "I've wanted to do that for a long time."

Scott held her close to him with his well-toned arms. "That makes two of us! But I should warn you I don't believe in making out or having sex until I get married. I think too much attention to the physical leads to trouble and can cloud a relationship emotionally. Or so my parents have told me, and I trust their judgment. I really like you, Rebecca, and I want to get to know you better but not in that way. Can you understand Princess?"

"I love it when you call me that, it makes me feel special, and you really are my Prince. I'm glad you don't expect me to hook up with you. I'm not ready for that yet either." Rebecca rested her head against his chest.

Scott held her for a few moments more and gently stroked her soft blond hair. "Thank you for being patient with me. I've never had a girlfriend before so this relationship stuff is all new to me."

"Oh, I'll let you know what to do and not do, my Prince. Believe me!"

"I believe you. I've seen how outspoken you can be. We better head back before our parents start to worry."

Rebecca grasped Scott's hand, and they walked back to the house. Everyone said their "goodbyes" and the Robinsons left. On the way home, Mrs. Robinson told Roger they were going to Paris with the Andersons in June.

"Do I have to go, Dad? Can't I stay here with friends?" Roger lamented.

"You're going, Roger! It will be good for you to see some place besides Whatcom," Mr. Robinson said.

"Oh, thanks Dad for letting Scott date me. He's just the kind of guy for me," Rebecca said.

"And he's the kind of guy I want you to date, the kind that will respect you and treat you well, and not some loser with sex on the brain," Mr. Robinson said.

"Scott wants to take me out next Friday to Rick's, is that okay?"

"No problem Sweetheart. Just be home before midnight."

"Cool, thanks, Dad."

After they got home, Rebecca immediately ran up to her room and texted Loretta to tell her the news.

"Scott finally asked me out!" Rebecca said.

"Awesome! I went out with Butch last night. We drank beer and made out at the park. He's a great kisser. I just wish he didn't smoke."

"Scott's a good kisser too, but he doesn't believe in making out. Do your parents know you're dating Butch?"

"No, and I don't want them to know."

"Are you sure it's a good idea to be involved with Butch?"

"Hey, I don't need a lecture from you. Can't you just be happy for me?"

"Loretta, I want you to be happy. I just think you can do better than Butch."

"That's easy for you to say now that you have your Prince Charming. So how was the barbecue? What's their house like?"

"Scott's house is huge. The moose burgers were delicious. I got to swim with Scott. He looks even better in a swim suit."

Rebecca paused, and then broached the subject of her upcoming trip to Paris.

"Oh, guess what? Scott's family invited my family to go with them to Paris in June."

"No way! You're like so lucky. Wish I could go with you."

"I can ask Scott and see if it would be alright. We could share a room. You'll need a passport, though. And, of course, your parents would have to approve."

"Please ask Scott. I'm sure if I begged and pleaded enough my parents will let me go, especially since there'll be plenty of adults around. So you want to go hang out at the park tomorrow? We can drink beer and eat sandwiches."

Rebecca hesitated. She was afraid to tell her friend why she didn't want to party in the park anymore like they used to do.

"I don't think that's such a good idea anymore. As minors, we're not supposed to drink beer. Besides, I'm planning to go to church tomorrow morning."

"Who are you and what did you do with my BFF?"

"Loretta I asked Jesus to be my Savior the other day, and now I don't want to do anything that wouldn't please Him."

"Oh no, you got religion! Well, keep it to yourself. I guess I'll see if Butch wants to party in the meadow since you're too self-righteous to hang out with your pagan friend."

"That's not true Loretta! I still want to hang out with you. I just won't be drinking anymore."

"Exactly, there goes the end of our fun together."

"You know that's not true. There are still things we can do that are fun. Scott and I will be at Rick's next Friday. We can all get together then. I better let you go, I heard my dad telling me to go to bed."

"Okay, goodbye Rebecca. I'll see you Monday at school."

Rebecca had a hard time sleeping she was so excited to have Scott as her boyfriend. She thanked God that night for bringing Scott into her life as she lay in bed. She was totally stoked to have a date with Scott finally. She also prayed for Loretta that God would save her. I hope she'll still want to be my friend. It would be a shame for my faith in Christ to break up our friendship. Where would I ever find another friend like Loretta?

CHAPTER 9

The Bully

The next morning, Scott texted Rebecca to ask her if she would like to go to church with him and his mom.

"I was planning to go to St. Paul's," Rebecca replied. "Let me ask my parents, though. I'd love to go with you. What church do you attend?"

"We belong to Whatcom Community Church; you know the big one on the outskirts of town. Talk to your parents and text me back. We'll get you in the Rolls. Shoot, your family is welcome to come too if they wish."

"Okay Scott, I'll get back to you."

Within a few minutes, Rebecca texted Scott back. "My brother and parents don't want to go, but my parents said I can go."

"That's wonderful! I'll be there at ten o'clock to pick you up."

Right on time, Daniel pulled in front of the Robinson house, and Scott went to the door to fetch Rebecca.

"You realize, Scott, a girl could get awfully spoiled riding around with you in that car all the time," Rebecca teased as they walked to the white Rolls-Royce.

"Good, you deserve to be spoiled, Princess, and I enjoy doing it," Scott said.

"Good morning, Daniel. Good morning, Mrs. Anderson," Rebecca said as she entered the car.

When they pulled into the church parking lot, Rebecca was surprised to see so many people there. The few times her parents had taken her to St. Paul's Episcopal in downtown Whatcom there was hardly anyone in the place except some of the town's oldest citizens. But this church seemed vibrant and alive like there was something wonderful happening.

They made their way to seats near the front. All along the way they were greeted by other church members, and Scott introduced Rebecca to them. She was amazed at how friendly everyone was towards her and equally surprised to see some of her classmates there. By 10:30 a.m. the worship team and pastor began the service. Rebecca quietly observed their joyful singing as she followed the words of each song projected on a screen in the front. Then the pastor began his sermon. Rebecca felt like he was talking directly to her, and followed his every word like a stray cat after a can of tuna. She felt like he was spoon feeding her heart. She loved this church.

"Pastor Fraser, this is Rebecca Robinson, my girlfriend," Scott said as he shook the pastor's hand by the front door after the service.

Rebecca was thrilled when she heard Scott call her his girlfriend.

"I'm very pleased to meet you, Rebecca. Say, isn't your father the owner of the sporting goods store?" Pastor Fraser asked.

"Yes, sir. I really enjoyed your sermon," Rebecca said as she shook his hand. "I'm kind of new to studying the Bible and you made it so much clearer to me."

"Thank you, young lady. I'm here to serve you. If you've any questions about the Bible, please call me." He handed his business card to her.

On the way back to Rebecca's house, a black SUV roared up behind them and tried to force Daniel to pull over. Seeming to sense the danger they were in, Daniel sped up and pushed a button on the dashboard, blasting the SUV with the rear EMP emitter, causing it to stop dead on the road. He quickly drove off.

"Yowza! That was scary!" Rebecca exclaimed. "What happened?"

"Daniel used an electromagnetic pulse to disable their car so we could get away," Scott said. "And if that wasn't enough, we have other means to defend ourselves against threats."

"That's good to know. Life is always exciting with you. I've decided I want to go to your church from now on. I just hope my parents aren't upset."

Daniel returned Rebecca to her home before taking Scott and his mom back to their estate.

During the week, Scott video chatted with Rebecca every evening to talk and to pray with her before they each went to sleep.

"Oh Scott, everyone can hardly wait to meet you," Rebecca said. "But now that I've accepted Christ as my Savior, Loretta and some of the girls don't want to hang out with me at school anymore."

"I'm sorry to hear that, Princess," Scott said. "I guess they're afraid of catching 'religion' like it was some kind of disease."

"It really hurts that Loretta avoids me now as much as she can. And Butch is really upset that you're dating me. So consider yourself warned—he will be gunning for you."

"I'm not too concerned about Butch. If he tries anything, he will soon learn not to mess with me. I haven't studied martial arts for nothing. Let's pray about the situation. 'Dear Lord, please be with Rebecca and help her to show Your love to her classmates in spite of their rejection. We especially pray for Loretta that you will save her, and help her to see that Rebecca can still be her friend. And we pray for Butch that you will save him. Please give us wisdom in dealing with these people Friday, in Jesus name, amen.' Good night, Princess."

"Good night, my Prince."

At last, it was that special Friday evening in mid-April. Rebecca watched out the window with great anticipation. Scott and Daniel pulled up to her house in the Rolls-Royce, and Scott came to the door.

"Come on in, Scott," Rebecca said. "Just let me get my purse and we can go."

"How are you doing, son?" Mr. Robinson asked from his easy chair.

"I'm doing well, sir. By the way, what time would you like me to bring your daughter home this evening?"

"I told Rebecca to be home by midnight. Thank you for asking."

Rebecca was wearing a pink dress, and Scott had a blue polo shirt on and tan slacks. Mrs. Robinson insisted on taking their photo before they left.

"You really do look like a princess; you're absolutely beautiful!" Scott said as they walked to the car.

"Thank you, my Prince. I see our usual 'carriage' awaits us," Rebecca said, smiling.

Before entering the vehicle, Daniel took their picture by the car. "Mrs. A's instructions," he said.

"Where to, Mr. Scott?" Daniel asked as they drove away.

"Take us to Rick's Diner, please, Daniel."

They drove a few blocks and then turned into the parking lot of the diner. There were already a lot of cars there. It seemed like everyone was there to meet Scott. Scott offered Rebecca his arm, and they walked into the restaurant like they were attending a state dinner. When they entered the diner, Rick himself came out from the kitchen and directed them to a booth by the windows. He removed the "Reserved" sign from the table, which Scott had apparently requested. All the kids in the diner were whispering to each other, likely about the couple. Then Loretta broke the ice and slid in beside Rebecca.

"Hi Scott, I'm Loretta Flannigan. Rebecca's told me all about you. OMG—you're hot!"

"You're welcome to sit here Loretta, but is that really what you want to do since you've avoided me all week?" Rebecca said. "And yes, Scott is hot."

Loretta ignored Rebecca's remark and just stared at Scott.

"I'm glad you ladies approve. Now, what would you like to eat?" Scott asked.

They each ordered some cheeseburgers and fries. One by one, Rebecca's fellow students came by their table to introduce themselves and to meet Scott, but they totally dismissed Rebecca. Then Butch showed up with his posse.

"Oh no, here comes Butch!" Rebecca exclaimed.

No sooner had she spoken those words than Butch barged into the diner with his friends close behind him. Everyone cleared out of his way as he strode over to Scott and Rebecca, grabbed a chair from a nearby table, placed it next to their table, and then straddled it.

"So this is like your new boyfriend, Rebecca?" Butch said, helping himself to Scott's fries.

"Hi, I'm Scott, and if you like fries so much I can have Rick bring you some," Scott said.

"Nah, I'd rather eat yours." Butch reached for more fries.

"I don't think so." Scott clasped Butch's wrist, preventing him from taking more fries.

Butch immediately stood up and took a swing at Scott's face, which Scott deflected with his arm, and then Scott used Butch's momentum to throw him onto the floor. Scott assumed a defensive posture. Butch looked bewildered, but when he came to his senses, he sprang up on his feet again.

"You know karate or something?"

"Yes, among other things."

"Well, let's see how you do with a Wolverine tackle!" Butch charged Scott.

Both guys went sprawling onto the floor.

Rick ran out of the kitchen with a baseball bat. "Get out of my diner, Butch!"

Scott returned to his booth and Butch stormed out the door, his gang following him. He pulled his pocket knife out and yelled, "Let's see how well they do with four flat tires!" Scott, Rebecca, and the others watched from the diner's windows.

Butch started to approach the Rolls-Royce with his knife, and Daniel jumped out of the car wielding his 45 caliber pistol.

"That's far enough young man!" Daniel yelled. "Now, place the knife on the ground and put your hands in the air."

Butch took a big gulp and complied with Daniel's demand. Daniel called the sheriff on his cell phone. Everyone watched as the sheriff drove up and saw his son standing in the parking lot at gunpoint.

"What's the meaning of this?" Bud demanded.

"This young man tried to flatten the tires of my employer's car with that there pocket knife." Daniel pointed at the knife on the ground.

"This young man is *my son,* Butch. Do you wish to press charges?" Bud asked. "Do you have a permit for that gun?"

"Yes, I have a permit, Sheriff," Daniel said as he holstered his pistol and produced the permit for Bud to examine. "And no, we don't want to press charges. I'm sure you're quite capable of dealing with your son's mischief."

"You bet I am!" Bud responded in anger as he took out his handcuffs and placed them on Butch. He then marched his son to the back seat of the patrol car like he would any other criminal.

"But Dad, what about my side of the story? Doesn't that count?"

"Son, if you're going to act like a criminal, I'm going to treat you like one. You can tell me your story from the jail cell in my office! Now get in the car and watch your head."

Cheers and applause erupted as the Sheriff drove off with Butch in custody. Everyone was happy to see Butch the bully get some payback because he wasn't very nice to anyone. But no one dared to cross him. Daniel returned to the car, and everyone patted Scott on the back for standing up to Butch. Even his gang went back into the diner to congratulate Scott.

"Dude, that was awesome the way you handled Butch!" Loretta exclaimed.

"That's my Prince!" Rebecca said. "Are you alright, Scott? Did he hurt you?"

"I'm okay, Princess. I guess Butch's reign of terror has come to an end for now," Scott said as he put a quarter in the jukebox controller at their booth and selected a romantic song. "When it comes to bullies, there are only a few things you can do. You can let them walk all over you, but appeasement will never change anything. Or you can fight them. The best way to deal with bullies is to stand up to them and to report them to those in authority. If you see someone being bullied, you have to tell someone who can come to their defense. It'll do nobody any good to remain silent. I knew Butch was deliberately trying to provoke me, so I had to stand up to him. But I was not about to stoop to his level. I just gave him enough rope to hang himself, as you all saw. I'd love to be a fly on the wall at the sheriff's office right now! I'm sure Butch is getting really chewed out by his father."

Everyone in the diner hung on every word Scott spoke. He was not only a hero in their eyes for standing up to Butch but a curiosity. They had never known any rich people and wanted to learn more about him.

"Scott, I bet your parents like buy you anything you want, right?" Loretta asked.

"Wrong. I work for my father and get a salary that I have to use for everything but my room and board. If I want new clothes, I have to buy them with my wages. My parents taught me how to manage money and the right way to use credit cards. And by saving up part of my salary, I was able to buy my car with cash. I have no car payments! I just have to pay for gas, insurance, and maintenance. And when I was a boy, my parents didn't just give me anything I wanted. I had to convince them something was good for me to have. And believe it or not, I'm glad my parents taught me how to use money responsibly."

"Whoa, you like have your own car and credit card. Sweet! I don't suppose you'd like loan me some money for new clothes," Loretta said.

"I could loan you the money, Loretta, but if you can't afford the clothes now how'd you ever be able to repay the loan? Do you have a source of income, a job or an allowance from your parents?" Scott asked.

"Yes, but it's not enough to buy new clothes."

"Then I would be happy to help you get a job or start a business to raise the money. Think about what you like doing and see if there is a market for it out there. That's how a lot of entrepreneurs got their start, and now some of them are multimillionaires."

"Wow Scott, you're not only good-looking but smart too. I'll have to think about your advice. Maybe I could provide a shopping service since I love to shop!"

"I'll vouch for that—this girl can shop with the best of them!" Rebecca exclaimed. "Scott, our baseball team has a game with the Lynden Lions next Friday, and afterward, there's a 'Sadie Hawkins' dance party. Will you be my date?"

"Of course! I can't speak for my dance skills, however. I have training in traditional ballroom dancing for my dad's company parties, but I'm not up on the latest dance moves."

"Awesome! You can pick me up at four o'clock, and we'll stumble through the dance together."

"And now, I have to work in the morning, so I better take you home. I enjoyed meeting all of you, and look forward to seeing you again next Friday."

"But it's only ten o'clock!" Rebecca complained.

"You're welcome to stay and find your own way home, but I was hoping to spend a little time with you alone before I have to go home."

"Oh, well then, goodbye everyone!" Rebecca motioned for Loretta to let her out of the booth.

Scott and Rebecca walked holding hands out to the Rolls-Royce, and Daniel promptly got out and opened the back door for them. He drove the few blocks to Rebecca's home and stopped in front of the house. Scott walked with Rebecca to the porch, and they sat on the swing. Scott put his arm around her shoulder and drew her closer to him. She leaned her head against him.

"I enjoyed our first date in spite of Butch," Rebecca said. "I'm just disappointed because I want to spend as much time as I can with you."

"I understand, Princess. I don't want to go either, but I won't be any good tomorrow if I don't get enough sleep. I'll pick you up for church on Sunday. We can spend the day together."

"I'd like that, my Prince."

"That's wonderful. Good night," Scott said as he leaned over and kissed her. Then he got up and went back to the car.

Rebecca just sat there for a few minutes after he and Daniel drove away. She was both excited and disappointed at the same time. She longed to be with Scott and treasured every moment they spent together. She also dreaded how Butch would react Monday at school, but she was determined to stand by Scott. Rebecca got up and went inside to find her dad sitting in his favorite chair, watching TV.

"How'd your date go with Scott, sweetheart?" Mr. Robinson asked. "You're home awful early, is everything alright?"

"Scott has to work tomorrow, so he brought me home early. Tonight was great. We got to see Butch get arrested by his own dad after Scott schooled him in the fine art of fighting without throwing a blow."

"What? Scott fought Butch?"

"Yes, Butch kept taking Scott's French fries, so when he stopped him, Butch tried to punch Scott. But Scott used his karate or something to defend himself. He never struck Butch. He just let Butch fall on the floor. It was so cool! Then Rick like kicked Butch out of the diner. So Butch tried to flatten the tires on the Rolls-Royce, and Daniel their chauffeur pulled his gun on him and called the sheriff, who arrested his own son. Scott said the only way to handle a bully is to stand up to him or to report him to the authorities."

"Sounds like you had an exciting evening sweetheart. Scott's right. I'm glad your boyfriend is not afraid to mix it up if necessary. It tells me he would come to your defense if the situation called for it."

"Yeah. I asked Scott to the dance next Friday, and he wants to spend the day with me this Sunday. Is that alright, Dad?"

"Yes, that will be fine, but would you ask Scott to come here for Sunday dinner after church?"

"Okay, Dad. Good night." Rebecca kissed her dad and went up to her room.

On Sunday, Scott rolled up to Rebecca's house in his midnight blue Porsche Boxster S convertible. Since a gentle rain fell, he'd left the optional hardtop on the car. Scott went to the door to pick up Rebecca, and they drove to his church for Sunday school and the worship service. Rebecca enjoyed the class on First Corinthians. She soaked in instruction from the Bible like a powder-dry sponge. Never before had the Bible been so clear to Rebecca. In some ways, it was like she had finally seen it for the first time. Afterward, Jake, the youth pastor introduced himself to her and encouraged Rebecca to come to their youth group meeting that evening.

"I think you'll enjoy it," Scott said. "We get to hang out with people our own age and play games, eat, and have our own Bible study. I promise we'll be done before your bedtime."

"Alright, but I better check with my parents first. I hope you're hungry because Mom and I are making something special for Sunday dinner."

"Oh good, I get to sample some more of your cooking."

Scott drove them back to her house, and he sat in the living room with Mr. Robinson while Rebecca and her mother finished preparing their dinner. Roger gazed out the window at Scott's car.

"Dude, you have like the coolest car! Did your dad buy it for you?" Roger asked.

"I'm not buying you a car Roger, so don't get any ideas," Mr. Robinson said.

"I bought my used car with my own money that I earned from working for my dad, Roger. Maybe your dad will let you work in his store to earn enough to buy a car."

"Dude, your dad must pay you well if you can afford a Porsche," Roger said.

"I make thirty-five dollars an hour and had to save up for a long time to buy that car. My parents got me a used BMW at first a couple of years ago, after I got my driver's license."

"I like the way you think Scott, but Roger doesn't even have his driver's license yet, and he's way too lazy to consider working for me. Of course, if you get desperate enough, Roger, you are always welcome to work at the store. Rebecca helps me out all the time."

"Dinner's ready!" Mrs. Robinson shouted from the dining room.

Everyone sat at the table, which was lavished with chicken parmesan, broccoli and cream cheese, fresh dinner rolls, Caesar salad, and sparkling cider.

"Wow! Everything looks and smells wonderful!" Scott exclaimed. "And I bet it tastes even better."

"Sis just wants to impress you, Dude. We don't normally eat this good," Roger said. "She even insisted we use the good china—is that lame or what?"

"That's enough, Roger!" Mr. Robinson said. "Let's say grace. 'God in Heaven, for what we are about to eat make us truly grateful. Amen.' Dig in, everybody!"

"Rebecca did most of the work Scott, I just supervised," Mrs. Robinson said.

"It's delicious. Your chicken parmesan rivals the best chefs in Italy, believe me," Scott said as he looked at Rebecca.

"Thanks, that means a lot to me. I've thought about becoming a chef since I love to cook."

"Then while we're in Paris in June, you should check out some cooking schools."

"I'd love that, but we could never afford it. It's always been my dream to study cooking in Europe. I want to open my own restaurant someday, or start a catering service."

"Rebecca, if God wants you to be a chef and study in Europe, He'll work it out. God can do things above whatever we could ever ask or think."

"You don't really believe that rot do you?" Roger asked with incredible snarkiness.

"Don't be rude, Roger!" Mr. Robinson scolded. "If you can't be pleasant, you can go to your room!"

"Roger, I'm sorry you feel that way, but yes, I do believe in God, and I believe the Bible is God's word to us," Scott said.

"And I believe it too," Rebecca said. "Knowing Jesus as my Savior has totally changed my life. I have a wonderful joy and peace of mind I never had before. And I feel like God is always there for me. You should try it, Roger."

"Oh no, not you too, Sis! Seriously, you've got religion? I should've known, since you're hanging out with Scott."

"We're happy for you sweetheart, just don't expect us to believe the same way. Roger, you should show more respect to your sister and Scott," Mrs. Robinson said.

"Look at the time!" Scott exclaimed. "If we're going to youth group this evening, we'd better get going."

"Mom and Dad, is it alright if I go with Scott?" Rebecca asked.

"Of course, honey. Just be home by ten. Tomorrow's a school day," Mr. Robinson said.

Scott and Rebecca left her home and returned to the church for the youth group meeting. Rebecca enjoyed it a lot. She felt so at home with the other young people, and Pastor Jake easily related to them. He made the Bible so practical in his lesson.

"Scott, do you think we could come to this youth group meeting every Sunday?" Rebecca asked.

"I can't promise you *every* Sunday, but sure we can make it a regular thing." He glanced over his shoulder. "Is it just my imagination, or has that black SUV been following us since we left the church?"

Rebecca turned to look at the vehicle about 200 feet behind them. Scott dropped her off at home, and once inside, Rebecca went to her room.

Lying in her pink and white bed, Rebecca thought about their conversation that day and resolved to become a chef. "Dear Heavenly Father, I want to be a chef," she prayed. "If this is what You want me to do with my life, then I trust you to make clear to me Your will and to provide the money for my training. Amen." Just as she was falling asleep, her cell phone rang.

CHAPTER 10

The Dance

"Hey Princess, I'm sorry to call you so late, but it's urgent that I talk to you. On the way home tonight, those men in the black SUV tried to kidnap me. They were even trying to shoot out my tires! Praise God I was able to outrun them and return home safely. But I'm afraid you, too, may be in danger because of your association with me. These people are ruthless and will do anything to extract secret information from my father's company about his AX-77 drone project. They may try to kidnap us to gain leverage over my dad so he'll give them the plans for this drone. I'm so sorry. I'm going to pay for a security detail to protect you. They'll arrive at your house, with me, in the morning to escort you to school and back. The sheriff and the FBI have been called about these spies. Please let me help you."

"Wow! Are you okay, Scott?"

"Yes, I'm fine. Daniel taught me defensive driving. If you would prefer I stop seeing you, I understand. I would never want to put you or your family in danger."

"Now that's something I'll have to think about, but it's not your fault these creeps are trying to kidnap you. I just find all of this a bit overwhelming."

"Alright. If you see anyone hanging around your place in a black SUV, call the sheriff right away. I'll see you in the morning, Princess. Let me know what you decide about us. Good night."

"Good night, my Prince."

Rebecca immediately got up and shared everything Scott had told her with her parents. Everyone was on edge, but no one was more fearful than Rebecca. She was afraid this could mean the end of her relationship with Scott before it had scarcely begun. Would she still want to date Scott if it meant putting herself and her family in danger? Then there was the fear of the unknown—would these guys break into their house and capture her? Rebecca whispered a prayer to God for protection and drifted off to sleep.

In the morning, Scott and his security detail arrived in a black, bullet-proof SUV and parked in front of Rebecca's house. Scott and one of the bodyguards came to the door.

"Good morning, Scott," Mr. Robinson said. "I appreciate you looking out for us like this, but I'm wondering if it would be better for you not to date my daughter until this matter is resolved."

"Good morning, Mr. Robinson. Good morning, Rebecca. If that is what you want, sir, I will respect that. But you should know I will always be in danger, from time to time, from industrial spies. The Chinese are desperate to get their hands on my dad's technology." He turned to the man standing next to him. "This is Vincent, and the man driving the SUV is Kelly. I have written down a password for Rebecca to use today with the security detail. If they can't tell you the password, you shouldn't go with them," Scott said as he handed an envelope to Rebecca. "Are you ready to go?"

"Yes. Can Roger ride with us, too?"

"Of course, there's plenty of room. Here—take this secure cell phone. It has the number you need to call when you're ready to go home. And don't forget to ask the guard for the password before you get in the vehicle from now on. I'll text you a new password on that secure cell phone every night for you to use the following day.

They all climbed into the SUV for the short ride to Whatcom High School. After dropping Rebecca and Roger off, the bodyguards returned Scott to the estate so he could meet with his tutors and continue to practice flying the AX-77 on the simulator.

It was the middle of April, and everything had gone smoothly all week.

"Hey Princess, how are you doing?" Scott said when he called Rebecca Thursday evening for their regular video call. "I got to go down to Edwards Air Force Base for a few days and fly the AX-77 UCAV, or Unmanned Combat Air Vehicle. It was like so much fun! I fired the laser cannons at fake targets and everything. My dad and Tom, his chief test pilot, thought I did a good job. I guess all my time in the simulator at home paid off. My dad wants me available as a backup pilot. You wouldn't believe the hoops I had to jump through to get a security clearance so I could help my dad with this."

"Sounds like *you* had a good week. I've got this whole security thing down to a routine, but nobody's seen those guys around town. Are you sure all this is really necessary?"

"Yes, it's better to err on the side of caution than to find out the hard way we didn't do enough. I would feel awful if anything happened to you. I really care about you, Rebecca."

"I care about you too. I discussed the matter with my parents, and we decided to go ahead and let you keep dating me for now since you have taken plenty of precautions to protect me. So—are you like ready for tomorrow night?"

"Since it's a 'Sadie Hawkins' dance, should I come in bib overalls?" Scott teased.

"No, silly. Just wear what you would wear to school for the baseball game, and if it's any help, I'm wearing my pink evening gown to the dance afterward."

"Okay, thanks. I'll see you at four. I'm pretty beat, so I'll say good night now, Princess."

Scott arrived in the Rolls-Royce the next afternoon, and Roger yelled up the stairs, "Sis, Scott's here!"

"Send him up. I'll be ready in a few minutes," Rebecca yelled back down.

"It's okay to come up, Scott," Mrs. Robinson called down. "I'm here doing Rebecca's hair."

In her mirror, Rebecca saw Scott timidly poke his head through the doorway to her room. She sat in a pink bathrobe, in front of her white and pink vanity, while her mother styled her hair. The walls had a pink, white, and pale green floral pattern on them. There was a white and pink desk with a mauve laptop on it. The white bookshelves were filled with all kinds of books on science and cooking along with some romance novels. On the other side of the room were two white doors for her closet and bathroom, and a white twin bed with many stuffed animals resting on a pink bedspread. Tucked next to the window was a small white telescope.

"So—what do you think of my room?" Rebecca asked.

"It definitely suits you. No one would have any trouble guessing what *your* favorite color is," Scott teased.

"Okay, young lady, I'm done," Mrs. Robinson said. "Now you two get out of here and have fun tonight."

Rebecca popped up, recovered a garment bag from the closet and handed it to Scott saying, "Here, make yourself useful. Carry this." She then whipped off her bathrobe, revealing a blue and yellow cheerleader's uniform underneath.

"What's with your outfit?" Scott asked.

"Oh, we on the cheer squad like to wear our uniforms to every sporting event."

"I learn something new about you all the time Rebecca."

Daniel pulled the Rolls-Royce up to the main entrance of the high school and Sam, the other bodyguard, jumped out to open the door for them. Scott and Rebecca grabbed their garment bags and went with Sam into the building while Daniel parked the car. Rebecca led Scott to the baseball field, and they found some seats in the bleachers near home plate. Sam stood nearby, keeping an eye on them. Rebecca ran off to the girls' locker room to stow her garment bag in her locker and then returned to her seat next to Scott.

They watched as the two teams warmed up on the field.

"Take this, rich boy!" Butch yelled as he hurled a baseball straight at Scott's head. Scott dived out of the way, and the ball struck the empty seat behind him. Sam had tried to catch the ball but missed. Scott recovered the ball and threw it right back to Butch's glove.

"Dude, what a throw! You should be on our team," one of the Wolverines players remarked.

"I can't join your team, but I'd be happy to work out with you sometime," Scott yelled back.

Butch looked visibly disappointed that he'd missed hitting Scott. But he wouldn't have too long to dwell on the matter. The Lynden High School Lions were ready to go. The Lions piled on the runs, inning after inning. The poor Wolverines didn't have a chance. No amount of exuberant cheering by Rebecca and the other students from the stands helped. The final score was sixteen runs for the Lions to the Wolverines' pitiful three runs. All the dejected Wolverine fans quickly left the bleachers while the Lions fans whooped and hollered on their way out to the parking lot. Rebecca directed Scott and Sam to a men's room for Scott to get into his tuxedo, and returned to her locker room to change for the dance. She met them by the entrance to the lunchroom in her pink satin evening gown. Loretta stood nearby, wearing a short, red prom dress.

The lunchroom had been transformed into an elegant ballroom, at least by Whatcom standards. All the tables and benches were moved to the outside walls, leaving the center of the room open for dancing. A spinning mirror ball hung from the middle of the ceiling, and blue and yellow crepe paper streamers radiated out from it to the walls. Interspersed were hundreds of blue and yellow balloons. The tables had blue plastic table clothes and centerpieces made of blue and yellow balloons and yellow carnations. A DJ played tunes in one corner of the room, and next to him was a long table just outside the kitchen, laid out with light refreshments, a punch bowl and, of course, blue and yellow plastic cups, plates, and napkins.

"Awe, the belles of the ball are here! You look quite stunning, Princess." Scott handed Rebecca a pink orchid corsage in a clear plastic container.

"Thanks, my Prince." She gave him a kiss on the cheek.

She pinned the corsage on, and they all entered the lunchroom. They found an empty table near the food. Sam stood nearby, against the wall, carefully observing everything.

"I'm sorry your team got blown out so badly," Scott said.

"That's okay, we're used to it," Rebecca said. "Lynden has always been tough on us."

"Of course, it would help if we had some better players like *you*," Loretta remarked. "I saw that throw you made to Butch before the game, Scott. Oh, there's Butch, now. I'm going to bug him."

"Come on, let's dance." Scott led Rebecca out to join the others dancing. "I'll try to keep up with everyone." Scott attempted to follow the other students' moves but seemed quite awkward. Rebecca bit her lip so she wouldn't laugh at his pitiful efforts.

"Would you like to learn how to swing dance, Rebecca? That's something I *do* know how to do."

"Okay, show me what you've got."

For the next few minutes, Scott taught her some simple steps for swing dancing, along with a few fancy flourishes. Soon, many of the other couples gathered around them, watching. They seemed to marvel at Scott's prowess on the dance floor. Most of them had only seen real ballroom dancing on TV.

Then the DJ switched to a slow song. Scott assumed the traditional ballroom dance hold with Rebecca and began to show her how to fox-trot. All the other couples just held each other close and swayed back and forth to the music. Then some of the girls turned their backs to their partners and started grinding up against them in an erotic way. When Rebecca tried to do that, Scott just turned and walked back to their table.

"Scott! Scott, what's wrong? Did I do something to offend you?" Rebecca called out as she followed him back to their table.

"I'm sorry, I can't be any part of such lewd behavior. It's not fitting for a Christian man to act that way with anyone but his wife, and then only in private. I forgive you, Rebecca. You're still just a baby Christian and don't know any better. There are even some ballroom dances I won't do such as the tango because they require moves that are way too sensual for unmarried people to be doing together. One of the things I greatly appreciate about you is that although you're incredibly beautiful, you usually dress quite modestly. Too many girls today show way too much skin, or cleavage, or both. I don't think they realize what they're doing to us guys. It's like waving a steak in front of a hungry tiger and not expecting him to want to eat it. Of course, I know there are other girls who know exactly what they're doing and dress that way deliberately to get a guy's attention. The point is it's not fair to guys, and it's demeaning to girls."

"I'm sorry, Scott. You know I would never do anything to hurt you. Do you really think I'm beautiful?"

"Duh! You look like a fashion model. But that's not the only reason I like you. Now that I've gotten to know you better, I appreciate the fact that you're also beautiful on the inside: intelligent and fun to be with. But most of all, you love the Lord now. These are all important qualities to me."

"Thanks. Am I blushing? I feel the same way about you. You're not only handsome and strong, but you're also quite smart, and a true gentleman. I'm happy that you're not like the other guys who just want to hook up with me. You know how to treat a lady with proper respect. And I always enjoy being with you, too. I just wish I had a way to show you how much I appreciate you."

Scott reached out and took her hands, stared into her blue eyes and said, "You already have, Princess, you already have. I'm glad you're able to carry on an intelligent conversation. Not all the women I've met are capable of that. But you can keep cooking dinner for me on Sundays if it will make you feel better."

Tears flowed down Rebecca's face as she got up and sat on Scott's lap to kiss him. For a few moments, he just held her close to him as she cried on his shoulder and tenderly kissed his cheeks. Rebecca wanted so much to show Scott that she was totally in love with him. He was just the kind of guy she could spend the rest of her life with. She would have married him on the spot if he'd asked her.

"Hey you two—break it up!" one of the chaperones yelled.

Rebecca complied and went to the other side of the table to dry her tears. Scott just smiled like a kid who'd been caught with his hand in the cookie jar. At eleven o'clock, the school principal told everyone to go home.

"Where are Loretta and Butch?" Scott asked.

"I don't know. They disappeared after our last dance," Rebecca said.

Scott escorted Rebecca out the main entrance with Sam in tow. Scott asked Daniel to take some photos of them in their formal wear before they got into the car. After they had arrived at Rebecca's house, Scott walked her to the door, kissed her good night, and once she was safely inside, returned to the car.

"How was the dance, honey?" Mr. Robinson asked from his favorite chair.

"It was great! Scott's a really good dancer—as long as it's ballroom dancing. He's pretty lame otherwise. We lost the game, of course."

"That's too bad. Maybe one of these years we'll get some better players. You look very pretty in that dress."

"Thanks. Good night, Dad." Rebecca kissed her father on the cheek and went up to her room.

"Did you have a good time tonight?" Mrs. Robinson asked after Rebecca entered her room.

"Yes, Mom, I did."

Mrs. Robinson sat down on Rebecca's bed beside her, and Rebecca melted into her mother's arms and cried.

"Oh Mom, I love Scott so much it hurts. I can hardly stand to be away from him."

"There, there, dear. Have you told him this?"

"No, Mom. I've told him how much I appreciate him, but I'm waiting to see if he loves me first."

"You're still young, dear, and have plenty of time. I know it's hard, but you should wait and see if this relationship is going to last. And if he really loves you, I'm sure he'll tell you when he feels the time is right. Just be patient. Scott's a good man and well worth waiting for. There are so few of them out there. But he's definitely a keeper. Your father and I both like Scott, too. So I hope everything works out for you two. Now, get some sleep. You have a house to clean tomorrow."

While Rebecca vacuumed the living room Saturday morning, her cell phone began to vibrate in her pocket. "Hello Scott, what's up?" Rebecca texted.

"Hi, just a quick note to let you know we won't need the security detail anymore. The FBI rounded up all the spies last night. We had quite a bit of excitement after I dropped you off. I'll tell you all about it at Sunday dinner."

"That's a relief! Alright, I'll see you Sunday. Thanks for keeping us in the loop."

Sunday, Rebecca made fried chicken, potatoes au gratin, and green beans for dinner.

"Rebecca tells me you had some excitement Friday night after the dance, on the way home, Scott," Mr. Robinson said.

"Yes, our 'eye in the sky' security helicopter spotted two black SUVs trying to box us in before we could return home," Scott said. "Sam stopped the SUV following by using the electromagnetic pulse emitter, or EMP, in the back of the Rolls. Then Daniel turned the car around so Sam could burn the gang members' hands with the laser cannons, causing them to drop their guns. We next snuck up on the other SUV, with our headlights off, and Sam blasted their vehicle with the front EMP, burning their hands, too, with the laser cannons. Those gang members were completely helpless as we drove past them. I'm glad I don't speak Chinese because I'm sure they were swearing up a storm."

"Dude, that's just like a spy car!" Roger exclaimed.

"Yes, my Dad bought that car the same time he got my Mom's 1957 T-Bird and had them both restored. However, since he was restoring the Rolls from the ground up, he added a few extra features such as armor plating and bullet resistant glass, bullet resistant tires, a more powerful engine with a turbocharger and better transmission, shielding for the EMP emitters so they don't fry the car's state of the art electronics, and two laser cannons in front. That 1977 Phantom Six is now one of the fanciest armored personnel carriers on the planet. In Daniel and Sam's hands, we can feel completely safe while traveling."

"We're just glad you're alright and that they got those guys. Now maybe we can relax," Mr. Robinson said.

"You'll be pleased to know, according to my dad, the FBI nabbed all of them, including some Chinese diplomats. They were immediately expelled to China with the understanding they will *never* be allowed into this country again. We still need to keep an eye out for anything suspicious, but yes, we can back off on the security detail for now."

"I wish I could tell Loretta all about this!" Rebecca said. "Speaking of which . . . I wonder what happened to her at the dance? She and Butch just disappeared before everyone left."

CHAPTER 11

The Mistake

After leaving Scott and Rebecca's side at the dance, Loretta bounded up to Butch and his buddies. They all sat in a dark corner of the lunchroom, near the door.

"Hey, Butch! You guys licking your wounds after Lynden whomped you?" Loretta said.

"Are you here to gloat and rub salt in those wounds, Red?" Butch asked.

"Who me? Would I do that?"

"Yes! You said you take fiendish delight in tormenting me."

"Nah, I just came to comfort you and see if you want to dance with me."

"I don't dance! But you look hot in that red dress, Red."

"Thanks. Come on, Butch; dance with me. I'll make it worthwhile."

Butch seemed reluctant as he left the table and joined Loretta on the dance floor. They just swayed back and forth to a slow song the DJ played. Loretta turned her back to Butch and began dancing up next to him in an erotic way.

"Now, isn't this worth it Butch?"

"Yeah, Red I like this. You're like so hot."

"You're not bad yourself. Listen, I know you guys did your best today against Lynden. They've always been tough to beat."

"That's right, we played hard and left it all on the field, but they still beat us."

"Maybe next time you'll do better. I saw how you tried to hit Scott with a baseball before the game."

"Yeah, too bad I missed. There you go, ruining the moment again, Red. Why can't you just shut up and let me enjoy dancing with you?"

"I'm sorry, Butch, I can't help it. I just like bugging you. It's only because I like you."

"Well, you have a funny way of showing it! I shudder to think what you would do if you loved me."

"What's wrong, don't you like your own medicine? You can dish it out, but you sure can't take it."

"Red, I think I'd rather stay sick than take any more of *your* medicine! Dance with someone else!"

"Oh, don't be that way, Butch. Let's get out of here. We can see if you can circle the bases and get a home run."

"Do you really mean it, Red?"

"Yes, let's sneak out now while everyone is watching Scott and Rebecca dance."

Butch drove to Lake Whatcom Park where they made out, and Loretta finally surrendered her virginity to Butch. She hoped it would encourage him to keep dating her. But she also felt terribly guilty afterward. It was not the most pleasant experience for her, but she was relieved to get it over with. Loretta thought sex would be more fun than that. Deep down, Loretta knew it was wrong, and she knew Butch didn't really love her, but at least he wanted her. And, she still wanted to be held in his strong arms. She was willing to give him sex just to feel like someone loved *her* for a few moments.

"That was fun, Red."

"Good, if you want to keep hooking up with me, you can't tell a soul. If I find out you were bragging to your friends, you won't be getting anymore of this!"

"Okay, Red, so when can we go out again? Next Friday?"

"I'll let you know by Thursday—if you've been a good boy. Good night, Butch."

"Good night, Red." Butch kissed Loretta, and she exited his truck at her usual drop off point.

Loretta walked home and soaked in her tub for an hour. So far, her plan had worked. Butch still wanted to date her. *But is it worth it? Have I done the right thing? Why do I feel so awful?* One thing was certain. Loretta knew she could never tell anyone she'd hooked up with Butch. Perhaps her parents were right. Butch was not the right guy for her. Still, she liked being with Butch. She enjoyed his attention and affection even if it was more to please him than her. Loretta determined to keep dating and hooking up with Butch. Perhaps in time the sex would get better, and Butch will come to really love her.

For the next two weeks, Loretta continued to date Butch and hook up with him regularly—at the park or any private place where they could steal a few moments. She began to enjoy the experience more but still feared that they would be discovered, or worse yet, that she might get pregnant.

"You brought protection, right?" Loretta asked as she and Butch sat in his truck at Lake Whatcom Park one Friday evening in late April.

"Nah, I'm out. Come on, Red, let's do it anyway," Butch said.

"No way! I don't want to get pregnant!"

"If you don't hook up with me now, I'll tell everyone in school what a slut you are, Red." Butch grabbed her arm forcefully.

"Stop, Butch! You're hurting me! Take me home now!"

"No. You're not going anywhere until you give me what I want." Butch slapped her face.

Shocked and terrified, Loretta began to cry. "How can you treat me this way? I thought you liked me."

"I'm sorry, Red. I do like you. But you can be so frustrating. Come here." Butch held her close to him and wiped away her tears with his hands as he kissed her cheeks. They made out, and Loretta finally relented and had sex with him.

As Loretta lay in her bed that night she began to wonder if dating Butch was such a good idea after all. *What if I get pregnant?* Her dad would kill her. *Butch never hit me before. Perhaps my parents and Rebecca are right. Butch really is a bad guy.* She knew what she had to do. She covered her pillow with tears at the prospect. She had to break up with Butch. But she didn't relish how he would react to the news. Loretta wondered if she would ever find a good man to love her.

On Saturday morning, Loretta came over to Rebecca's house. When Rebecca opened the door, Loretta said, "Hi Rebecca, can we talk?"

"Does this mean I'm no longer *persona non grata*?" Rebecca asked.

"I don't know what that means, but I'm here to tell you I'm sorry for ignoring you. I want my BFF back."

"Good! I missed you, Loretta." Rebecca gave her a hug. "Let's go up to my room and we can talk."

Both girls walked upstairs to Rebecca's bedroom and sat side by side on her bed.

"What did you want to talk about?" Rebecca asked.

"I want you to know I don't resent your being religious. If that's what makes you happy, good for you. But I hope you can accept that I don't believe the same way."

"Loretta, I love you so much that I honestly hope someday you will have the same inner peace and joy that I have, but I'm not going to force my beliefs on you. I just hope you can also respect my new lifestyle. Scott and I pray for you daily. We want you to be happy, too."

"I do respect you, Rebecca, and I love you, too. But when you told me about your new religious views, it tore me up. I felt like I had lost my best friend. But after having a few weeks to think about this, I just can't toss all our years of friendship in the trash just because you've changed."

"I forgive you, Loretta. But it really hurt me when you and the other girls shunned me."

Loretta was relieved her friend was so understanding. She was not sure she could ever be that forgiving! It was clear Rebecca had changed into an even kinder, gentler person. Loretta envied what she had, but wasn't willing to 'get religion' to have it. She bolstered her courage to tell Rebecca about her and Butch.

"Thanks, again I'm like, so sorry. You'll be happy to know I've decided to break up with Butch. You were right. He's not a nice guy. The other night he hit me when I wouldn't have sex with him."

"Oh no! Loretta, have you told Butch's dad that Butch hit you? What he did is illegal. He should be in jail for assault!"

"I can't do that. I'm afraid my parents will find out, and I'll get in trouble. I'm also afraid of Butch. That's why I've been avoiding him at school."

"Come here." Rebecca embraced her. "Would it help if we confronted Butch together?"

"I think I need to do this on my own. Thanks, Rebecca, for giving me another chance. You really are my BFF."

"And you're mine. I'll be praying that things will work out right with you and Butch."

"How are things going with you and Scott?"

"Great! I'm like so in love with him. I really think Scott could be the one for me, Loretta."

"I'm happy you finally found a great guy, Rebecca. I'd better get home and do my chores."

As she helped her mom with the laundry, Loretta was so glad to have Rebecca as a friend again but didn't feel comfortable telling even her that she had had sex with Butch. *What am I going to do if I'm pregnant? I don't have the money for an abortion.* Loretta knew what she had to do, but didn't look forward to it at all. She resolved to avoid Butch as long as possible so she wouldn't have to confront him.

CHAPTER 12

The Mission

"Finally tonight," Pastor Jake said to the youth group Sunday evening after the dance, "In First John chapter three, verses seventeen and eighteen, we read, 'But whoever has this world's goods, and sees his brother in need, and shuts up his heart from him, how does the love of God dwell in him? My little children, let us not love in word or in tongue, but in deed and in truth.' This is another test John gives us of whether we truly have saving faith. How well do you show love towards others, especially believers, in practical ways? In keeping with this, I have a challenge for you. I'll let Sean O'Brian explain it. Come on up, Sean."

"Thanks, Pastor Jake," Sean said. "As some of you know, my mother and I regularly volunteer at the mission in Bellingham. I talked to Pastor Jake, and we would like to form a team from our youth group to help out at the mission. We would mainly be working in the kitchen on Saturday, preparing and serving meals.

You will need a Washington State Food Handler's card and must go through orientation. I made some flyers explaining everything and how to get a card. So if you're interested, please see me afterward."

"That sounds like something I can do," Rebecca said. "We should go together, Scott."

"You can go if you wish, but I doubt if I would be of much use in their kitchen," Scott said. "I don't know anything about cooking."

"Oh, come on Scott, it will be fun. I can show you what to do."

"Rebecca's right bro, it's not hard to serve food to needy people. We can show you what to do. Or are you too much of a momma's boy to serve Christ this way?" Sean playfully slugged Scott on the arm.

"Alright, alright, you win!" Scott said. "My arm can't take being twisted by both my girlfriend and my best friend. But don't say I didn't warn you. My mom never lets me do anything in her kitchen."

"Great! Here's some flyers for you and Rebecca, bro," Sean said. "Let me know when you have your food handler's cards and we will set up a time for you to serve at the mission."

"By the way Rebecca, this is *my* BFF. Sean and I have been pals ever since he moved here from New York and joined the youth group. I will need your help to get a card."

"Why don't you come over tomorrow after school and we can both apply together? Bring your laptop," Rebecca said. "This is going to be fun, serving at the mission."

The next day, Scott came over to the Robinson home, and Rebecca helped him with the online test to get a food handler's card. Once they both had their cards, Scott called Sean to set up volunteering at the mission the following Saturday.

On a Saturday near the end of April, Scott and Rebecca went with Pastor Jake to the mission.

"Here's an apron, plastic gloves, and a hair covering," the food service manager at the mission said. "You can start by peeling those potatoes and chopping them up into chunks for the beef stew."

After Scott and Rebecca were properly dressed, Rebecca washed all the potatoes and said, "Take this peeler and remove the skin from the potatoes like this, and then place them in this bowl. I'll remove the eyes and any icky parts. When we finish that, I'll show you how to chop them up."

"Yes, Your Majesty," Scott said.

Rebecca carefully observed Scott peeling the potatoes. "No, no, no, Scott! You want to just barely take the skin off. You're cutting away too much of the potato!"

"Maybe you'd better show me again."

Rebecca took the peeler and once more, demonstrated how to use it. "Now, you try it. Just skim the surface enough to remove the skin. That's right; now you've got it!"

When all the potatoes were peeled and ready to be chopped up, Rebecca took a French cook's knife and showed Scott the most efficient way to cut them into chunks.

"First, cut the potato lengthwise into quarters, then hold it together and rock the knife up and down on the cutting board about every half an inch. Voila! You'll be able to cut it up into chunks quickly."

"You make it look so easy, Rebecca. I don't think I can do it as fast as you."

"It's not a race, Scott. Just take your time until you get the hang of it."

"Whacking potatoes is kind of fun. I see why you like cooking so much. You get to torture food!" Scott assumed a menacing pose. "Hee hee, you shouldn't have done it. Now I'll have to cut you up," he said, acting like a crazed killer as he brought the knife down on a potato. "Take that, you naughty potato."

Rebecca laughed. "You crazy, silly man!"

"Crazy about you, give me another potato to torture."

When they finished with the potatoes, the food service manager gave them some carrots to peel and chop up. Rebecca washed them, too, and instructed Scott to peel them the same way he had the potatoes. "Now chop off both ends and just as we did with the potatoes slice the carrots into thin slices—like this." Rebecca quickly rocked the knife up and down on the carrot.

"Oh boy, more food to torment!" Scott said.

After they had finished with the carrots, it was time to serve lunch to the guests. The food service manager put Scott and Rebecca on the serving line, dishing out soup and sandwiches. Rebecca was moved by how appreciative the guests were for the meal. She was grateful for the opportunity to serve Christ and to work in the mission kitchen. She also gained a greater appreciation for how good she had it living with her parents. She had so much compared to these people. *But for God's help, I might be homeless. I should teach Scott how to cook since his mother won't do it.*

On the way home, Rebecca asked Scott, "Since you're going off to college next year, would you like me to show you how to prepare some simple meals?

"Nah, that's what takeout is for."

"Maybe *you* can afford to eat restaurant food every day, but it's not very healthy. I can show you how to fix some healthy dishes that don't cost much, either."

"Nah. Did you enjoy serving at the mission today, Princess?"

"Yes, I did. I think I want to volunteer there some more. It's a good way to serve God and it will look good on my resume. Why won't you let me teach you how to cook?"

"Because I just don't think it's necessary. I'll always have someone else to cook for me."

"You really are a momma's boy. I'm disappointed in you, Scott. You're too proud to cook anything yourself and expect others to wait on you hand and foot. You're spoiled, Scott. From now on if you wish to eat Sunday dinner with me, you're going to have to help me cook it!"

"Then I guess I won't be eating Sunday dinner with you anymore."

"Seriously, you would rather forgo eating Sunday dinner with me than have to spend time in a kitchen? I rest my case—you're too arrogant for your own good. Is that how Jesus would act?"

For the rest of the drive home, Scott didn't say anything. He completely shut down. Rebecca was so angry with him. All she'd wanted to do was help, but he was too proud to accept it.

As they pulled up in front of Rebecca's house, Scott said, "You're right, Princess. I'm spoiled. I didn't see it until now. I have so much more than most people have. And you're right that I'm too proud to accept your help. It's not how Jesus would act. I'm sorry, will you forgive me?"

"Yes, my Prince, I forgive you. Please let me help you."

"Okay. I guess it wouldn't hurt me to learn how to do a few things. It would save me time and money in the long run when I go to college. So I'll humble myself and let you teach me how to cook."

"Good, you can have your first lesson tomorrow after church." Rebecca kissed Scott and went into her home.

Right after they arrived at the Robinson home after church on Sunday, Rebecca gestured with her finger to bid Scott to follow her into the kitchen. "Come with me, Scott, we have work to do."

Like a lamb going to the slaughter, Scott reluctantly followed her. "If I must, your wish is my command. But I'm afraid any attempt by me at cooking is going to be a disaster."

"Don't be afraid, Scott. I will walk you through each step. I have something for you that my mom and I picked up yesterday." Rebecca handed Scott a royal blue bib apron. "Put it on so you don't mess up your clothes. I also printed out these recipes of simple dishes. Do you like tuna casserole? We can make it with either rice or pasta. Which would you prefer?" Rebecca tied her lacy pink bib apron around her waist.

"Thanks for the apron, Princess. I've never had tuna casserole, but I would prefer rice."

"Okay, before we get started I just have to get a photo of us." Rebecca took out her cell phone and snuggled up next to Scott to take a selfie. "The first thing you need to do is start the rice." Rebecca handed Scott a sauce pan and a box of rice. "Have you studied chemistry yet? Cooking is a lot like chemistry, except you don't have to be quite as precise with the measurements. Put about an inch of water into the saucepan and place it on the stove. Next, put a dash of salt into the water to make it boil faster, and turn that knob to medium high. Now, pour out just half a cup of rice into this measuring cup. Here's where you don't want to use too much rice, or it will spill over. I usually use the 'pinch and dump' method when I cook, but since you're a rookie, we'd better measure things out." She watched as he followed her directions. "That's right, Scott, pour the rice in the water and stir it a little with this wooden spoon and then place the lid on the pan."

Rebecca thought it was so much fun to be cooking with Scott. Especially since he felt uneasy about doing it. He looked so cute in that apron, fumbling about in the kitchen.

Scott carefully followed her instructions. "How will we know when the rice is done?"

"It will be all puffy and soft. Alright, now let's get the other ingredients ready. Besides a couple of cans of tuna, we can add all kinds of things to jazz up the casserole. For example, you can chop up some onions or garlic or green peppers, whatever you like. You can add frozen peas and carrots and sprinkle grated cheese on top. This way, you have a well-balanced meal in just one dish. So—what do you want to do?"

"They all sound good to me. Let me get this straight. We mix all this together in one dish? How do you cook it?"

"That's why it's called a casserole. When the rice is done, we will place everything in this casserole dish and bake it in the oven for about thirty minutes. The beauty of it is while you're waiting for it to bake, you can be studying or doing homework. Now, let's get everything ready. The rice won't take very long to cook." She watched as he picked up an onion. "You will want to stand back when you chop the onions, or you will be crying like a baby."

Scott held the knife at arm's length to cut the onions. Then he tackled the green and red peppers.

"Be careful to remove all those little seeds. That's right. Now, open two cans of tuna with this can opener and then drain the water off."

Scott fumbled with the can opener. Rebecca showed him how to do it with the first can of tuna and then handed the can opener back to Scott.

"Okay, pour these peas and carrots into this measuring cup, clear to the top, and then take this grater and grate some cheese into a bowl while I check the rice."

"Cool! Shredded cheese, do we get to mush it all together yet?" Scott grappled with the cheese and the grater while Rebecca drained excess water off of the rice.

"Yes. See how fluffy the rice is? That's how you know it's done. Now, pour everything but the cheese into this large mixing bowl and 'mush it all together' as you say. When you're done, we can scoop it into the casserole dish, add some cream of mushroom soup to the mix, and sprinkle the cheese on top. Then it will be ready to bake in the oven."

"I can see you'll make a great chef because you're so good at bossing people around."

"Talk about the pot calling the kettle black! I'm not the only bossy one around here."

"Is dinner ready yet? I'm starving," Roger complained from the living room.

"It will be done in thirty minutes," Rebecca said.

While the casserole baked, Rebecca showed Scott how to make a salad and to set the table. At last, everyone gathered at the table for Sunday dinner.

"Scott made the casserole with my help," Rebecca said. "I'm teaching him how to cook before he goes away to college next year."

"Dude, this is good! I wasn't sure at first if I wanted to eat it or not," Roger said.

"Thanks, Roger, I had an awesome teacher," Scott said. "This is really good, Rebecca. And you're right. It wasn't that hard to make. There may be hope for me yet."

"Good, look over the recipes I gave you and tell me what you want to try next," Rebecca said.

"We should have you teach Roger how to cook too," Mr. Robinson said. "Then he can help out more in the kitchen."

"Oh, Dad, I don't think that's such a good idea," Roger said. Roger pushed his dirty plate toward his sister, who pushed it back and frowned at him.

"Then you can wash all the dirty dishes young man," Mrs. Robinson said.

"Okay, Rebecca can teach me to cook if I don't have to wash dishes."

"Who's ready for dessert?" Rebecca said. "I made a chocolate cake yesterday." She hoped everyone liked it. It was a recipe she'd found in a cooking magazine. If she could bake more and more difficult things, maybe she *could* be a chef!

"Yum, please cut a slice for me. I don't have to learn to bake cakes, do I?" Scott said.

"Not yet, that's a little too advanced for you. Baby steps, Scott, baby steps. Dad, are you still going to take me to my driving test this week?"

"Yes, sweetheart, I will make sure you get tested this week."

"Awesome! If I pass, I'll finally have my driver's license."

"Oh no, look out world. Sis is coming to a street near you," Roger said.

"I bet I'm a better driver than you, you brat."

"Okay, you two, knock it off," Mr. Robinson scolded. "Roger, you can clear the dishes and wash them since Scott and Rebecca cooked. And if I hear a word out of you, you'll be washing dishes all week."

To Rebecca's great delight, they each finished every crumb of cake on their plates. She was on her way. But would her parents allow her to go to cooking school instead of college?

As a perfect conclusion to the day, at the youth group meeting that evening, Rebecca arranged to ride to the mission the next Saturday with Pastor Jake and the other young people, since Scott had to work for his father.

True to his word, Mr. Robinson took Rebecca to her driving test on Wednesday.

"Guess what?" Rebecca said when she called Scott to video chat that evening. "I passed my driving test! I now have my driver's license." Rebecca waved her license in front of the phone.

"Congratulations, Princess! I'm so happy for you."

"I have a favor to ask you. All my driving lessons were with cars that have automatic transmissions, so could you like teach me how to drive a stick shift?"

"Sure, no problem. Will Saturday afternoon be okay?"

"No, I promised to help at the mission with the youth group that day. What about Sunday after dinner?"

"That will be fine. By the way, I want to learn how to make macaroni and cheese Sunday."

"Good! See you Sunday, my Prince." Rebecca was delighted that Scott wanted to learn how to cook now. And she was relieved that he was willing to show her how to drive with a stick shift.

On the following Saturday, Pastor Jake picked up Rebecca with the church van and they met Sean and his mother at the mission. They were planning to help in the kitchen that day. After they had finished serving the evening meal, they all walked back to their vehicles in the parking lot. Three young men approached them.

"Yo, hand over the keys to the van and all your money. And you girls get in the van. You're coming with us."

Rebecca slipped into the van and immediately called the police while Sean and Pastor Jake stepped towards the three gang members.

"Look, we don't want any trouble!" Sean said as loud as he could. "Here this is all the money I have, but you can't have the van or the girls."

All the thugs pulled out guns and pointed them at Sean and Pastor Jake. "You better give us what we want, boy, or I'll cap you," the leader of the thieves said.

"Dude, I'm not afraid of you. I'm a child of the only true and living God and yes, you may kill me, but how do you think God is going to feel about you killing one of his kids?" Sean said.

Before the gang members could respond, twenty big homeless men carrying pipes, sticks, and baseball bats surrounded the muggers.

"You punks best back away and leave these good people alone if you don't want a beat down," Charlie, an older guest at the mission, said.

The three gang members slowly backed away, tucked their guns back in their pants, and ran down the street just as two police cruisers showed up to chase them down. A third police car rushed into the parking lot.

"Thanks, guys," Sean said to the men who'd come to their rescue.

"You're welcome, kid. We may be homeless, but we'll always have the backs of those who take care of us," Charlie said. "I don't think those three punks will be giving you any more trouble."

Rebecca was still in shock at what just happened, and how close to death Sean had come. The police took everyone's statements and then let them leave.

"I can't believe how Sean stood up to those guys," Rebecca said as Pastor Jake drove them home. "And then how all the residents of the mission ganged up on them. That was scary. Praise God; we're all right, and no one got hurt."

"I'm not at all surprised by Sean's actions," Pastor Jake said. "He used to be in a gang in New York. He knows how they think.

All the guys at the mission would give their lives to protect us. Charlie was right, they protect their own, and since we're helping them, they are very protective of us."

"After what happened, I hope my parents still let me volunteer at the mission," Rebecca said. Rebecca wasn't sure she even wanted to tell them or Scott what happened.

"If they object, let me talk to them Rebecca," Pastor Jake said. "I can assure them it's perfectly safe. The guests will escort us to our vehicles, if necessary."

When Rebecca returned home, she explained to her parents what had happened and urged them to let her keep going to the mission. She also texted Scott that evening.

"Sounds like you had an exciting day, Princess. I was praying for you."

"Yes, that was way more excitement than I care for. Thanks for praying. It was awesome and scary how Sean and the mission residents stood up to those gang bangers. I managed to calm my parents' fears, so I can still volunteer at the mission."

"That's good. You got to see firsthand how God can protect you."

"Yes, I suppose I did. In my head I know I can trust God to protect me, but when it's happening it's hard to get my heart to do anything but panic."

"Hey, there's nothing wrong with being afraid. It's how you handle that fear that counts. Are you going to trust God or let your fear cripple you? Speaking of which, are you ready for your driving lesson tomorrow?"

"Yes, are you ready for your cooking lesson?"

"Of course, and I have a surprise for you. See you in the morning, Princess."

Rebecca wondered what Scott had up his sleeve. She was relieved her parents would still let her cook at the mission. Maybe Scott would let her drive his Porsche. That would be so much fun!

CHAPTER 13

The New Driver

Rebecca was a little disappointed on Sunday morning when Scott drove up in a different car instead of his Porsche.

"Good morning, Princess! Are you ready to go to church?"

"Yes, but where's your Porsche?"

"It's back home. Since I'm giving you a driving lesson this afternoon after Sunday dinner, I brought my old 2003 BMW 325i. This is my first car. It's still a sweet ride."

"Bummer, I was hoping to drive the Porsche."

"Baby steps Princess, that's way more car than you can handle right now. Maybe someday, after you have more experience, you can drive my Porsche."

When they returned from church, Rebecca let Scott try to follow the recipe for macaroni and cheese on his own, with little instruction from her, while she prepared a meatloaf to bake at the same time. When everything was done, they all gathered at the dinner table.

"This mac-n-cheese is delicious. Nice and cheesy, and your meat loaf is good too, Rebecca." Scott took another bite.

"Thanks, you did a good job following the recipe. Now, can you see how this will help when you're on your own at college?"

"Yes, thanks for your help."

"Do you know what college you're going to yet?" Mr. Robinson asked.

"I've applied at MIT in Boston but haven't heard back from them yet."

Rebecca didn't want to think about Scott going clear across the country to college. She would miss him too much!

"Somebody has a birthday coming up," Mrs. Robinson said.

"Oh Mom, I don't need a lot of fuss," Rebecca said. *I wonder what my parents will do for my birthday?*

"When is your birthday?" Scott asked.

"It's on May fifth, and don't get any bright ideas about having a fiesta or something just because it falls on Cinco de Mayo. My mom already tried that when I was six."

"Okay, got it, no fiesta. But you can expect me to do something to celebrate your birthday. Now, not to change the subject Mr. Robinson, but I was wondering if Rebecca could come with me to my dad's fancy party next Sunday afternoon? He's invited some important people to meet with him at home, and I would enjoy it more if Rebecca were there to keep me company. He expects me to be there. Otherwise, I'd rather be here with you."

"We don't have a problem, Scott, if Rebecca wants to go," Mr. Robinson said.

"Thanks, Dad. I'd love to go, Scott, but I don't have anything fancy to wear to the party. Do you think we could run over to Bellis Fair Mall in Bellingham this week?"

"No problem, how about Friday night?"

"That sounds good. Would you mind if Loretta came with us? She has such great fashion sense!"

"Okay, I'll pick you both up right after school. We can grab supper at the food court. Now please pass me some of your delicious cherry cobbler. And then—it will be time for your driving lesson."

After dinner, Scott drove them to the Anderson Aerospace parking lot by the Bellingham airport.

"Okay, Princess let's switch places, and we can begin. No one is working here today, so we have the parking lot all to ourselves." Rebecca and Scott changed places. Rebecca was quite nervous sitting behind the wheel of Scott's Beemer.

"Before you start the engine you should familiarize yourself with a few things. Make sure your seat and mirrors are adjusted properly. You see that pedal on the left? That's the clutch pedal. You need to be able to depress it all the way to the floor."

Rebecca adjusted the seat and mirrors until she was comfortable. She felt like an elephant trying to walk on raw eggs without breaking them. She didn't want to do anything to ruin Scott's car. "Alright, now what do I do?"

"Look at the gear shift. See where each gear position is? Depress the clutch pedal all the way and practice moving the gear shift from first gear to all the others before you start the car."

"Like this, Scott? I'm so afraid of messing up your car."

"Don't be nervous. You can't hurt this car too much. That's why I brought my old car. And to give you a little added incentive, if you do well today, I'll let you borrow this car to use."

"Seriously? I can have this car to drive? That would be so awesome! I could drive myself to the mission to get experience working in a professional kitchen."

"Yes. Okay, now put it in first gear and start the engine. Don't forget to take off the parking break. Give it a little gas and slowly ease up on the clutch pedal."

Rebecca tried to follow Scott's instructions but the car lurched forward, and the engine died.

"Try it again. This time, let up the clutch more smoothly as you depress the gas pedal."

Rebecca started the car again and that time, she was successful at getting it into first gear. They slowly rolled forward in the parking lot. She was thrilled! Success at last!

"Now, drive to the end of this row and turn around. Remember, when you stop, you need to hit both the brake and the clutch, or you'll kill the engine. Good, good . . . now you're getting it."

Rebecca managed to get to third gear by the time they'd reached the end of the row, but she forgot to depress the clutch when she hit the brakes and killed the engine again. "I'm not doing so well, am I?"

"Princess, you're doing fine. It takes time to learn to coordinate everything smoothly. Try again, but this time put it in reverse, back up to turn around, and then put it in first. Go to the end of the row, downshift, turn around, and come back."

Rebecca complied with Scott's direction and that time, she was able to successfully make all the gear transitions. Soon she was driving all around the parking lot at thirty-five miles per hour and successfully down-shifting with each turn. "This *is* a fun car to drive, Scott. I'm really getting the hang of it."

Boom! Rebecca slammed on the brakes as the right front tire blew out. "Oh no! What happened? I've wrecked your car."

"You must have run over some debris in the parking lot. The front tire is flat."

"We should call someone to help. I'll call my dad. He'll know what to do."

"That's not necessary. We'll just change the tire to the spare in the trunk. This will be another learning experience for you. Now you get to learn how to change a flat tire."

"Really? You can do that?"

"Yes, pop the trunk with that lever." They both got out, and Rebecca watched as Scott showed her how to change a tire. He let her remove some of the lug nuts and then tighten them after the spare tire was installed.

"I can't believe it. We were able to change the tire just like that. Even I could do it. Thanks for showing me this."

"No problem. Of course, now I'll have to take the car with me today so I can get that tire repaired or replaced, but I'll bring it back for you to use once I'm done. I think you're ready to hit the streets and try the freeway. I want you to see what it's like to get this baby up into fifth gear."

"Are you sure, Scott? Do you really think I can handle actual driving on the street?"

"Yes, come on let's go."

Scott told Rebecca how to get back to I-5 from the airport, and he had her drive south to the last exit before leaving Bellingham, turn around, and come back to the Mount Baker exit to return to Whatcom. By the time they reached the church that evening for youth group, Rebecca was easily driving the Beemer. After the meeting, they sat in the car in front of her house for a few minutes.

"Thanks, my Prince, for the driving lesson. I feel a lot more confident driving a stick shift. And thanks for letting me use your car. I promise to be very careful with it. I know about guys and their cars. You never forget your first love."

"You're right; Brunhilda does have sentimental value. I got many a speeding ticket when I was sixteen, in this car. My parents wouldn't let me buy the Porsche until I cleaned up my act."

"I never knew you were such a speed demon. Do you name all your cars?"

"Yes, my Porsche is called Matilda. Good night, Princess." Scott kissed Rebecca, and she went into her home.

Rebecca was so glad that Scott trusted her enough to let her use his old Beemer. She immediately sent Loretta a text with the news before she went to bed.

When she came home from school Monday, Brunhilda was parked in front of her house, sporting a new tire. Apparently, Scott had dropped it off during the day. Her dad gave Rebecca the keys and urged her to be very careful with Scott's car. Even though it wasn't very far away, Rebecca drove Brunhilda to school each day, with Loretta riding shotgun.

On Friday, Rebecca drove her and Loretta home in the Beemer, but when they arrived, they saw Scott and Daniel waiting in the Rolls-Royce. Loretta seemed quite impressed with the Rolls as they took the twenty-minute drive to Bellis Fair Mall in Bellingham.

"Dude, you weren't kidding about how cool this car is!" Loretta said. "It's like totally awesome! I can see how someone could get quite spoiled with a ride like this."

Daniel dropped them off by Macy's and then parked the car to wait until Scott summoned him. Rebecca and Loretta went through all the racks of formal dresses and picked out a few that they both agreed would look good on Rebecca. Rebecca tried them on and came out to get Scott and Loretta's opinion. They all finally settled on a pink, sleeveless, floor-length dress with a scoop neckline and lace and rhinestone decorations on the bodice.

"You look great in anything Rebecca, but I like that dress," Scott said. "It's just the right mix of fancy and tasteful, modest and stylish. It's like so *you*. Now it's your turn Loretta, my treat. Get something you can use for the next prom."

"Shut up! Do you really mean it?" Loretta asked.

"Yes, knock yourself out," Scott said. "You told me you wanted some new clothes, so now's your chance."

Loretta didn't waste any time choosing a few dresses to try on. It was like a Loretta fashion show. She finally decided to get a sleeveless, red, floor-length dress with a ruffled strap for the halter neckline.

"Oh Loretta, that dress really goes well with your red hair," Rebecca said. "Now we just need some shoes to match our dresses."

"Alright ladies, lead the way to the shoe department," Scott said.

For the next thirty minutes, Rebecca and Loretta tried on tons of shoes that matched their dresses before each picking a pair they liked. Scott settled up with the clerk, and they headed toward the food court.

"I'll catch up with you later at the food court, guys. I need to get something," Loretta said.

"Okay, we'll see you later," Scott said.

Scott and Rebecca casually walked hand-in-hand to the food court, gawking at the displays in the store windows. They found an empty table and piled their bags onto one of the chairs. Scott left Rebecca there to hold their table while he went to pick up some food for them. He returned with two steaming containers of rice and teriyaki chicken.

"So, like who all is coming to this dinner party your dad is having?"

"Most likely all of his top executives, board members, some politicians and important military generals with their wives or girlfriends. This is an annual event my father hosts, so it's like a great honor to be invited. Who knows? Maybe the Washington State Governor will show up too."

"Wow! This party really *is* a big deal. Are you sure you want a small-town girl like me there?"

"Yes, Princess, I do. Everyone will love you. Besides, once we schmooze a little with the guests, we can go off somewhere and hang out. And you can never place enough value on getting to know important people. Someday it may pay off to know some of these people. I talked with your dad, and I have a surprise for you."

"Oh yeah, what's the surprise? When did you talk to my dad? Why?"

"If I tell you, it won't be a surprise. All I can say is your dad gave me permission to take you somewhere all day on your birthday. Believe it or not, he's letting you ditch school that day to go with me."

"He must really trust you to let me skip school on my birthday. Come on, tell me. What's the surprise?"

"Sorry Princess. My lips are sealed."

"Well—maybe I could unseal them with a kiss." Rebecca moved closer to his face and kissed him.

"You're welcome to try, but it won't do any good."

"Hey, get a room!" Loretta barked as she came up to their table and dumped all her bags on an empty chair. "Can you watch these while I get a burger? Thanks." And off she went to purchase her meal. When she returned, Loretta slumped into a chair and asked, "So what'd I miss?"

"I was just trying to persuade Scott to tell me what he and my dad are up to. Scott conspired with my dad to let me skip school on my birthday and spend the day with him."

"No way!" Loretta remarked. "Your dad's letting you ditch school on your birthday? Wish my dad would let me do that. So where are you taking her, Scott? Maybe tickling will get him to talk." Both girls began to tickle Scott.

"Sorry girls, I'm not ticklish, so you're wasting your time. All I can tell you is we're going down to Seattle, and you will like it a lot. Now, I'd better call Daniel and get you both home; they just announced that the mall will be closing in ten minutes."

Daniel met them outside Macy's where he'd dropped them off and drove to Rebecca's house. Loretta walked across the street to her home while Scott said good night to Rebecca. Then Scott and Daniel returned to their car and left for the Anderson estate.

Saturday, whenever she got a chance, Rebecca tried to pry more information about her birthday out of her dad, but he wouldn't tell her anything she didn't already know.

Sunday after church, Rebecca and Scott changed into their formal clothes at the Robinson home. Mrs. Robinson insisted on taking photos of them for herself, and Scott had her take some photos for him, too. He drove them to the Anderson estate for the party. Scott went directly into the garage with his Porsche while all the guests were being dropped off at the front door. They rode the elevator up to the fourth floor.

"Why are we coming up here?" Rebecca asked.

"Because I wanted you to be able to make a grand entrance. Haven't you ever dreamed about how cool it would be to come down a curved staircase in front of a crowd like they do in the movies? I want the whole world to know that you're my Princess."

"Scott I don't think this is such a good idea. I'm nervous enough without making a spectacle of myself. Please, let's just go down to the party in a less conspicuous way."

"Very well, but I still think it would be fun to show you off."

Rebecca wondered if Scott, too, just liked her just for her looks. She had no desire to become some guy's trophy wife. They got back in the elevator and went down to the main floor, where they met up with Mr. and Mrs. Anderson, who received their guests by the front door.

"Oh Rebecca, honey, you look stunning and like a catfish out of water at the same time," Mrs. Anderson gushed as she gave Rebecca a hug.

"Thanks, I feel very much out of my element here."

"Just try to relax, dear. You'll get used to this sort of thing in time. If this small-town girl from Georgia can get used to it, so can you. Remember, darlin', people are people from the penthouse to the outhouse."

Scott stood next to his parents in the reception line with Rebecca by his side. He introduced her to all the guests as they arrived. Rebecca was amazed and honored to meet so many important people all in one place. There was a steady stream of business leaders, sports stars from Seattle, celebrities, politicians and even the governor showed up for a brief time. Rebecca even got to meet the owners of some popular restaurants in Seattle. They all gave her their business cards. After about thirty minutes of conversing with the guests, Scott spirited Rebecca off to the rec room. There, they found some men in the billiard room and other guests milling around the pool outside.

"Let's go hang out in the flight simulator," Scott suggested. "It'll be quiet in there, and we can talk."

"Can we fly it, too?"

"Certainly. Are you sure you're up to that?"

"Show me what you got, flyboy."

Scott helped her into the flight simulator and strapped her in, and then took a seat beside her. He closed the door, and the din of the party was gone. Scott powered it up and selected the biplane version with a simulated French countryside setting. Away they went as he took off from a field. He started out gentle at first and then began doing aerobatic maneuvers such as loops and barrel rolls. He even flew under a bridge!

"OMG!" Rebecca exclaimed. "This is like so much fun! It's like being in a real plane, but it must look really strange to be flying in formal wear."

"Do you want to try flying, Princess?"

"Can I? That'd be like so awesome!"

Scott placed her hand on the stick between her legs and said, "You use this stick to control the ailerons and elevators, and the pedals on the floor to control the rudder. Pull back on the stick to go up; push forward to go down; push the pedals to go left or right. Okay, it's all yours."

Rebecca carefully tried each of the controls until she got the hang of it. Then she began banking the simulated plane to turn left and right. Finally, she did a couple of spins and a loop before Scott took the controls again and landed the simulated plane.

"This is so much fun I'd love to go up in a real plane sometime."

"I'll talk to my dad and see if he'll let me use his Stearman biplane. I don't know about you, but I could use some food. I'm famished!"

"Food sounds good. I'm glad we didn't eat first, or I might have barfed all over your simulator!"

Scott shut down the simulator. After climbing out, he lifted her out of the simulator and onto the floor. They walked out on the patio, grabbed some plates, and selected from the many choices on the buffet tables. Scott led Rebecca over to one of the tables set up beside the pool, and they sat down to eat.

"Who's your caterer? This is delicious! Perhaps someday your mom will let me cater this party."

"I don't know, but I can ask my mom. I hate to be a killjoy, but if we want to go to youth group this evening, we'd better take off. Or we can skip it this Sunday and just hang out here. Your choice."

"I don't want to miss youth group, but I also don't want to leave. Thanks for bringing me Scott. I wasn't sure about all this highbrow stuff, but I've actually enjoyed the party."

For the rest of the evening, they sat out by the pool and talked until it was time to take Rebecca home. She wondered if this is what it would be like to be married to Scott—a life of fancy parties and exotic locations around the world. Or would she be in constant danger from industrial spies? Would Scott have to travel all the time, like his dad did, and leave her home by herself? Is that the lifestyle she could expect if they got married? Rebecca hoped not. She wanted to be able to see her husband on a daily basis. That was something she needed to know if their relationship was going to last.

At ten o'clock, Scott ran her home in his Porsche. Rebecca had a hard time sleeping that night. She was so excited about what Scott had planned for her birthday. *Maybe we'll get to go up in the Space Needle. He must really like me to go to all this trouble for my birthday. I wonder if Loretta has broken up with Butch yet?*

CHAPTER 14

The Breakup

Monday the first week of May, Loretta was retrieving some books from her locker when Butch showed up.

"Hey Red, I haven't seen you for a while. Are you deliberately trying to avoid me?" Butch said.

"Yes, Butch I am. I can no longer see you. You're not good for me." Tears began to roll down Loretta's cheeks. She remembered how painful their last date was and how much it hurt her to say goodbye to Butch.

"Red nobody dumps me! I decide when this relationship is over. If you don't keep dating me, I'll tell everyone what a slut you are."

"News flash Butch, I just did dump you! And everyone already knows we hooked up." Loretta brushed the tears from her face and shook her finger at Butch. "Furthermore, Rebecca was right. You're nothing but a selfish, abusive, irresponsible bully! I honestly hope you grow up someday and learn the right way to treat a lady. No girl with any sense would want to date you! I was a fool for thinking we could ever make it together! We're done, Butch! Deal with it!" Loretta stormed off down the hall to her next class leaving Butch standing there in stunned silence in the midst of the crowd that had gathered to see their very public breakup.

Within minutes, Loretta saw on her phone that someone got video of the incident. It quickly went viral. All the girls, especially those dumped by Butch, rallied to support Loretta. Even Butch's own teammates on the baseball team wanted nothing to do with him. Butch was a social outcast.

That evening Loretta was in her room doing her homework and reflected on what happened. She knew she made the right decision. But it still hurt. In a way, she felt sorry for Butch, but he brought it on himself. Now he was getting his own medicine in spades as all the cyber bullies piled on the abuse. Will I ever find the right guy? So far none of the other guys at school have shown any interest in me. After what happened with Butch, I'm waiting until a good man comes along, someone who will treat me right.

Loretta's cell phone buzzed on her end table. It was a text message from Scott.

"Hi Loretta, Rebecca told me what happened today. You did the right thing. We want you to know we're praying for you. I'm sure God has just the right guy out there for you, Loretta."

"Thanks, Scott, that means a lot to me. I hope you're right. But after what happened with Butch, I can't help but have my doubts."

"Anyway, I need you to do something for me."

"Whatcha need?"

"As you know Rebecca's dad and I are planning to surprise her for her birthday Friday. I've reserved Rick's for a surprise party that evening. What I need you to do is tell all her close friends about the party. Everyone needs to be there by five o'clock. I'll let you know when we're on our way that day so everyone can be ready."

"I'll be happy to help Scott."

"Oh, whatever you do make sure her brother Roger doesn't know until after we leave for Seattle Friday morning. It would be just like him to try and spoil the surprise."

"I know what you mean; that kid's a first class brat. I'll take care of it, Scott."

"Okay, thanks. Good night Loretta. See you Friday."

"Goodnight Scott. Rebecca is going to be so surprised!"

CHAPTER 15

The Birthday

Thursday night before her birthday, Scott asked Rebecca to be ready to go by 7:00 a.m., to dress casual and bring a warm coat and gloves.

As expected, Scott rang the Robinson's doorbell at seven o'clock Friday morning. Surprisingly, Rebecca was ready to go. It was a gloriously sunny May day with hardly a cloud in sight, so Rebecca did not understand why Scott asked her to take a coat and some gloves along, too. They drove to Bellingham and caught Interstate 5, southbound. Rebecca barely noticed they were flying down the freeway at 70 miles per hour in Scott's Porsche. He turned on his stereo system and began playing some contemporary Christian music. *I love this music!* She'd never realized there were so many capable Christian artists out there. The music was comparable to any pop song but with cleaner lyrics.

"I've got to put these songs on my MP3 player!" Rebecca said. "I feel like singing praise to God along with them."

"Then go ahead, Princess."

Rebecca's soft, sweet, soprano voice blended with the song coming from the speakers. Scott's baritone soon joined her voice. For the next forty-five minutes, they sang together, until they reached the outskirts of Everett. Scott stopped to devote his full attention to the heavy traffic caused by people commuting to work. By nine o'clock they were driving past downtown Seattle. Rebecca gawked at all the tall buildings and the Space Needle. She had seen photos of the skyline, but it was even more impressive to see it in person.

"I thought you said we're going to Seattle? Why are we driving past it?"

"We'll go there after your surprise. First, we have to go to Tukwila."

Scott exited off I-5 by Southcenter Mall and drove to a business park consisting of two-story beige buildings. He pulled into the parking lot by one of them, and Rebecca noticed the distinctive bright blue and white logo near the top of the building.

"OMG! Le Cordon Bleu! I never knew they had a school here in the U. S. You're the best boyfriend in the world!" Rebecca threw her arms around Scott's neck and gave him a big kiss.

"Actually, they have campuses all over the world and not just in Paris. I've arranged for you to have a tour for your birthday. That's why we had to come down here during the school day."

Rebecca was totally stoked. The lobby had light colored hardwood flooring and a table displaying students' exotic looking cakes. A receptionist's desk stood behind a tall counter.

"Good morning, I'm Scott Anderson, and this is Rebecca Robinson. We're here for a tour," Scott said to the young woman at the reception desk. "I made arrangements with Admissions."

The receptionist called the office upstairs, and they were soon joined by a middle-aged woman with shoulder-length black hair.

"Good morning, Scott and Rebecca!" the woman greeted them. "Welcome to Le Cordon Bleu! If you'll come with me, I'll show you our facilities."

For the next twenty minutes, she led them into the various kitchens on the first and second floors. They watched as students scurried around preparing food on massive stainless steel counters as well as with professional stoves and ovens. Rebecca was fascinated with it all. She was looking forward to attending this school. Finally, they went into the Admissions Office. The woman handed Rebecca an information packet with all the paperwork she would need to apply for admission, financial aid, and everything else she might need. *Yikes!* Rebecca's eyes widened when she saw the tuition prices. She hoped she could get some financial help. Otherwise she could never afford this school. She might have to give up on her dream.

"We have two certificate programs; each takes nine months to complete, including experience with local businesses. Do you have any questions?"

"Not at this time. This place is like so cool! I'm not sure how I'm going to pay for this, but we'll find a way. I'll look over the information you gave me. Thanks for the tour."

After they had returned to the car, Rebecca began to cry. "Scott, this is so wonderful, but how will I ever be able to pay for this? My parents want me to follow my dream, but they aren't made of money."

"Remember, Princess, if God wants you to come here for school, He will work everything out perfectly. Just do your best and let God do the rest."

They left the school and went up to Seattle where they spent the rest of the morning at Pike Place Market looking at all the shops and watching the fishmongers toss fish to each other to impress the shoppers. Scott took Rebecca up in the Space Needle for lunch. Afterward, it was time to return to Whatcom. Once again, Scott turned on the stereo as they drove back.

"Scott, when is your birthday?"

"August first. Are you plotting to get me back?"

"Oh, you never know. I doubt if I could top this. You know that I want to be a chef, but what are your plans for a career?"

"I want to be an aerospace engineer, and also get an MBA like my dad did. Someday I hope to take over as CEO of my dad's company. But, God willing, it will be many years before that happens."

"Does that mean you'll seldom be home, like your father?"

"I hope not. I want to be able to enjoy my family every day. I love the idea of waking up each morning to see my wife and children. That's what I like about your family Rebecca. Your dad is home every night after work. Don't get me wrong. I love my parents. But I spend more time with my mom and Daniel than I do my father. I don't want my children to go through that."

Rebecca was greatly relieved to hear Scott say that. Still—saying it was one thing, doing it was quite another.

When they reached Bellingham, Scott drove to the airport. He pulled up next to a large hanger with the Anderson Aerospace logo on it.

"What are we doing here, Scott? Does this mean what I think it means?"

"If you think it means we're going flying, you're right! My dad said I can take you up in his Stearman biplane. You'll need your coat and gloves, however." Scott removed them from the trunk of his car.

Now she understood. "Awesome! How long have you had your pilot's license, Scott?"

"I started taking lessons when I was sixteen and got my license after I turned seventeen last August. I've been flying every chance I can get since then."

After they had entered the hanger, Scott handed Rebecca some blue coveralls. Once they were in their coveralls and coats, Scott strapped a parachute on her back. He donned his own parachute and opened the hanger door. Scott fueled the blue and yellow biplane and then got some guys to help him wheel it outside. He grabbed two helmets, which he placed inside the two open cockpits, and did his preflight check around the airplane. Finally, it was time for them to climb aboard.

Scott helped Rebecca into the front seat and got her strapped in, with her helmet and goggles in place. Rebecca was starting to get hot. After Scott was strapped in, he started the engine and checked all his instruments and control features. Rebecca felt the blast of cool air from the propeller wash over her, much to her relief, and could hear Scott talking on the radio with the tower. The plane's engine was loud as Scott let the big radial engine warm up for ten minutes. The tower directed Scott to taxi out to the runway and wait for his turn to leave.

Rebecca felt anticipation building as they sat by the end of the runway. At last, the tower gave Scott permission to take off. He maneuvered the plane onto the runway and throttled up the engine. The roar was deafening. Soon, they zipped down the runway and left the ground as Scott gently pulled back on the stick. As they slowly gained altitude, Scott slammed back the throttle lever and the stick, causing the plane to shoot up in the sky at a steep angle. When the altimeter indicated they were around two thousand feet in the air, Scott leveled off the plane and banked it towards the east. He flew over Bellingham and Whatcom. Rebecca looked down on her hometown. It looked so tiny. She could see her high school soccer team practicing on the field. Scott pointed out his family home as he banked the plane around to head back west.

When they were over Puget Sound, Scott asked over the radio, "Are you ready for some excitement?"

"Go for it, flyboy!"

"Okay, here we go." Scott went into a series of barrel rolls followed by a couple of loops and up into a hammerhead. Rebecca screamed her head off the whole time.

"OMG! That was like intense! Let's do it again!"

"Your wish is my command, birthday girl." He guided the plane through a series of aerobatic maneuvers for the next ten minutes. While doing a hammerhead, the engine stopped. The plane began to go into a dive. Scott managed to pull it out of the dive and level the plane, but now they were just gliding towards the water of Puget Sound, below.

"Oh no, what do we do?" Rebecca asked.

"Take the controls and hold the plane steady while I try to restart the engine."

Scott pressed the starter button and tinkered with the engine controls. After a few attempts, the 450 horsepower Pratt and Whitney engine roared into life again. Scott grabbed the stick and brought them back up to 2000 feet.

"Yikes!" Rebecca exclaimed. "That was close. I thought for sure we were goners."

"Yes, Princess, it would have put a real *damper* on your birthday if we'd crashed in the water."

Rebecca groaned at Scott's attempt at humor.

They had been in the air for almost an hour. Scott checked his watch and the fuel gauge. "It's time to head back to the airport." He contacted the tower for a landing approach. Scott banked the plane to line it up with the runway and brought it down onto the tarmac. He taxied back to the hanger, turned the plane, and shut off the engine. They climbed out and quickly removed their helmets, parachutes, coats and gloves. Rebecca grabbed Scott and kissed him. For a few minutes, they embraced inside the hanger.

"I'm so glad we didn't crash into the water. Thanks so much for this, Scott. This has been like the best birthday ever."

"I'm glad we didn't crash, too. My dad would be very disappointed if we'd wrecked his plane. It's an honor, Princess, to take you flying for your birthday. I'm happy you enjoy flying. Now—I need to put away the plane, and then we can head back to Whatcom for supper."

Scott once again got some men to help him back the Stearman into the hanger. After everything had been put away, they got back into the car to return to Whatcom.

"Can you find me a restroom? All that flying put a strain on my bladder."

"No problem, Princess." Scott drove to the nearest gas station.

While Rebecca was using the restroom, Scott sent a text message to Loretta letting her know they were on their way.

When Rebecca returned, Scott wasted no time driving to Whatcom and went straight to Rick's Diner. Rebecca thought nothing of all the cars in the parking lot. She assumed it was the regular supper crowd. But as soon as they entered the diner, everyone stood up and yelled, "Surprise!" Rebecca was totally taken back. She'd never suspected for a minute that there was a party waiting for her. It was completely overwhelming.

"Thanks, everyone! This is like so awesome! Best birthday ever!" Rebecca exclaimed, tears running down her cheeks.

Rick brought out some burgers and fries for Rebecca and Scott. They'd been seated at a table in the middle of the room, along with Mr. and Mrs. Robinson, Roger, Mrs. Anderson and Loretta, while everyone else went back to eating. In between bites of food, Rebecca related everything she and Scott had done during the day.

Once everyone was finished eating, Rick brought out a birthday cake with white frosting and pink roses iced everywhere. Seventeen pink candles further embellished the cake. Rick wheeled it up to Rebecca on a kitchen cart. Mrs. Robinson and Mrs. Anderson both took photos of the cake and Rebecca while everyone sang, "Happy Birthday" to her. She took a deep breath and blew out all seventeen candles. Everyone applauded her effort. Rick cut a big piece of the chocolate cake for her before wheeling it back to the counter to serve the others.

"This cake is delicious, Rick!" Rebecca said. "You did a great job. Thanks!"

Loretta leaned over to whisper. "Rebecca, can I sleep over with you tonight? I desperately need some BFF time. My parents said its okay."

Rebecca turned to her parents. "Mom, Dad can Loretta sleep over tonight? Please?"

"Yes, since tomorrow's Saturday," Mr. Robinson said.

"Thanks, Dad." Rebecca gave Loretta a knowing look.

Around eleven o'clock Rick said, "Alright everyone the party's over. I need to close up."

Scott and his mother left together after Scott kissed Rebecca goodbye. All the Robinsons and Loretta crowded into Mr. Robinson's Bronco and went home. Rebecca and Loretta immediately ran upstairs to her room and began getting ready for bed.

"You should have seen Le Cordon Bleu, Loretta; it was like way cool. I definitely want to go there after I graduate next year if God provides the money."

"You're like so lucky, Rebecca, to have Scott for a boyfriend," Loretta called out from the bathroom.

Rebecca climbed into her bed and waited for Loretta to finish in the bathroom.

"Oh no! Shut up! It can't be true," Loretta cried. She emerged from the bathroom totally convulsing with sobs, tears pouring down her face.

"What's wrong?"

Loretta gasped for breath. All she could do was hold up a positive home pregnancy test stick. The color drained from Rebecca's face, and she rushed to comfort her friend.

CHAPTER 16

The Crisis

Rebecca wrapped her arms around Loretta, and they both collapsed onto the floor beside her bed.

"Breathe, Loretta! Slow and steady! Nice, deep breaths."

Loretta leaned her head against Rebecca's shoulder and sobbed until she regained some composure. Rebecca stroked Loretta's curly, red hair.

"How did this happen?" Rebecca asked. "I thought you were going to wait until you got married?"

"Please don't judge me! What am I going to do? If my parents find out, they'll kill me."

"I'm not judging you. I just want to know what happened."

"If you must know, Butch and I have been hooking up. When I was late, I got a home pregnancy test while we were at the mall in Bellingham, and hid it from my parents until I could use it, here away from them. That's one reason why I wanted to sleep here tonight. I've got to get an abortion. Do you think Scott would loan me the money and take me to the clinic?"

"I don't know. We can always ask. I have an idea. Let's have a picnic tomorrow at the meadow and invite Scott. Then, you can ask him after we eat. My mom says it's always best to talk to men about important stuff after they have had a good meal." Rebecca got her cell phone and texted Scott right away.

"Hi, it's me. Loretta and I are having a picnic tomorrow in the meadow. Do you want to come?"

"I have to do some work for my dad tomorrow morning, but I think I could meet you there by noon. Good night, Princess."

"Good night, my Prince. Scott's coming at noon! We'd better get to bed so we can get up early and make something scrumptious for the picnic." Both girls climbed into the bed and talked well into the night before falling asleep.

In the morning, they quickly got dressed and worked together to finish Rebecca's chores. Then, they prepared the mother of all picnic baskets. Loretta told her parents she would be home in the afternoon after the picnic to do her chores. Around ten o'clock, Rebecca drove them to the park, in Brunhilda. They laid everything out in the middle of the meadow, on a blanket, and waited for Scott to show up.

"Did you ask Scott if I can go to Paris with you?"

"Yes, he didn't see a problem with us sharing a room as long as your parents approve and you have a passport."

"Then I guess I'd better get one quick. Have you got your passport, yet?"

"Not yet, but my dad says they should be ready soon. When Scott gets here, I think you should let me do most of the talking at first, and then I'll let you take over."

"Okay, you know Scott better than I do."

Each girl helped herself to the cut-up carrots and celery. Rebecca earnestly hoped their plan would work. "So what was it like hooking up with Butch?"

"It was both painful and wonderful. What about you and Scott?"

"We haven't hooked up and don't even make out. Scott made it clear from the outset that he was waiting until marriage and didn't want to emphasize the physical in our relationship. He's affectionate, but just doesn't want to like dwell on it, and that's fine with me."

"Sounds like you've met your match, then."

"You're right, Loretta. If Scott asked me to marry him, I wouldn't hesitate to say, 'Yes.' I love him so much it hurts. And I agree with him that the best wedding gift I can give my future husband is my virginity."

"Looks like I blew that gift exchange. Now I'll be lucky if any man wants me."

"That's not true, Loretta. You're still a wonderful girl, and any man would be lucky to have you as a wife. Just because you blew it with Butch doesn't mean you can't abstain from sex until you get married. I think Scott calls it 'secondary virginity.'"

"Good afternoon, ladies!" Scott called out as he walked up to them. "Looks like you have a pretty good spread." He flopped down on the blanket next to Rebecca and greeted her with a kiss.

"What would you like? We've got fried chicken, potato salad, Chinese pasta salad, some cut up veggies, sweet pickles, soda, and one of my famous apple pies for dessert."

"I'll take a little of everything. I can see why you like this meadow, it's quite serene. Can we give thanks first, before we eat?"

They joined hands while Scott prayed a simple blessing over the meal. Rebecca prepared a plate for him, and the girls helped themselves to the food, too. After they had finished eating, Scott lay back on the blanket and gazed up at the sky. Rebecca sat beside him and began stroking his wavy black hair as she looked deep into his eyes. Loretta sat next to Rebecca.

"Scott, Loretta needs your help with something. It would mean a lot to me if you would hear her out and consider her request. Go ahead, Loretta."

"What do you want, Loretta?"

"Scott, I'm pregnant, and I was like wondering if you could loan me the money for an abortion. I can't let my parents know about this or they'll disown me. If it would help, you can return the dress and shoes you bought me. Please help me Scott; I'm desperate."

Scott sat up abruptly, and asked Loretta, "Are you sure you're pregnant? Who's the father? Have you told him?"

"I took a home pregnancy test last night, and it turned out positive. Butch and I have been hooking up, but he doesn't know I'm pregnant."

"I see," Scott said. "Loretta, it's not a sin to be pregnant. The sin is in *how* you got pregnant. And it would be a greater sin to kill an innocent baby just to cover up sleeping with Butch. Besides, there is a risk, if you have an abortion, that you might never be able to have children again. Worse, you could die from complications. I really think you need to see a doctor to be sure you're pregnant, and if you are, you need to tell Butch and your parents."

"But isn't it a woman's right to choose to have the baby or not?" Rebecca blurted out. "And who says it's a baby yet? It's too early for it to be anything more than a blob of tissue."

"First, there's abundant scientific evidence that human life begins at conception," Scott said. "And second, what about the rights of the baby—to life? God places a high premium on human life because we are created in God's image. Just because the law of the land says you can murder your unborn child doesn't make it right."

"But Loretta still needs help. Isn't there something you can do to help with an abortion?"

"I'm sorry you feel that way about abortion, Rebecca. I can't help Loretta if it means aiding in the death of a baby. I guess I don't know you as well as I thought, Rebecca, and I deeply resent you manipulating me like this." Scott promptly got up and ran across the meadow to return to the parking lot.

"Wait here, Loretta," Rebecca said and ran after Scott.

She arrived at the parking lot just in time to see Scott drive away. Rebecca trudged back to the meadow, crying uncontrollably. She collapsed on the blanket into Loretta's arms. "He's gone, Loretta. Scott's gone. I think I just blew it big time. But how could he just leave like that? He's usually very kind; how can he show no compassion for you? Maybe I should just let him go if he's going to act that way."

"Hey, are you just going to give up? I've seen what you two have, and it's worth fighting for. You need to go talk to him and try to work things out. Don't worry about me. I'll figure something out."

"You're right, Loretta. I can't give up. I have to see if we can reconcile our differences. Let's take this stuff home and drive over to Scott's house."

Rebecca drove up to the front door of the Anderson estate and Mrs. Anderson answered the door.

"Why hello, Rebecca. Who's your little friend?" Mrs. Anderson said.

"This is my best friend, Loretta. I brought Scott's car back. I was hoping I could talk to him, Mrs. Anderson."

"Come on in, girls. I was just about to have some tea. Can I get something for you?"

"Your house is like ginormous!" Loretta said. "Do you have any soda?"

"Yes, dear, I think we have some in the refrigerator." Mrs. Anderson led the girls to the kitchen, and they sat at the table while she fixed some tea and fetched the girls a glass of root beer for each girl. "Scott has been in his room ever since he got back from your picnic. He was very upset. Is there something you want to tell me?"

"I think I really hurt Scott," Rebecca said.

"We tried to get Scott to pay for my abortion," Loretta said.

"I see. Does that mean you're pregnant, Loretta?"

"I think so. I took a home pregnancy test last night, and it was positive."

"It sounds like you all need to talk this out with my son. I'll get him."

Mrs. Anderson went upstairs and was gone for a long time. Finally, she and Scott came into the kitchen. "Loretta, honey, why don't you stay here with me and let these two go somewhere to talk?"

Scott and Rebecca left the kitchen and went downstairs to the rec room.

"You really hurt me, Rebecca."

"I'm sorry, Scott. I never meant to hurt you. I just hoped you could find a way to help Loretta. Surely there must be something you can do."

"Rebecca, given the way you feel about abortion, I don't think there's anything more to talk about, and I'm no longer sure we should be together. I still care about you and want to be your friend, but I can't be your boyfriend anymore. This is a deal breaker for me. I can't be in a romantic relationship with a woman who believes in killing babies."

"And I can't be in a relationship with a heartless man. So maybe we should break up. Scott, I don't know what I believe anymore when it comes to abortion. Remember I've been fed all this stuff in school about abortion for years, and I never heard your side of the story before. I thought about what you said, and I want to do what would honor God. But right now I know that my best friend needs help. If you have any ideas that can help Loretta, I want to hear them. And I'm sorry we tried to butter you up with the picnic. Can you forgive me? I brought Brunhilda back."

"Yes, I forgive you, Rebecca. But I think we need to take a step back. You can keep using my Beemer."

"And what about Paris? I suppose if we break up that's out of the question."

"No, my family made a commitment to take your family to Paris with us, and I think we should honor that. So you can still come with us. Maybe it will help us sort out what kind of relationship we really want. And you're right, of course, I should have more compassion for Loretta. I've thought and prayed about her situation and have some ideas to share with her."

"Good! Let's go back and discuss them with her."

Scott and Rebecca walked back upstairs to the kitchen and sat down at the table with Loretta and Mrs. Anderson.

"Loretta and I had a good talk while you two were away," Mrs. Anderson said. "She has something to tell you. Go ahead, Loretta dear."

"I just asked Jesus to save me," Loretta said. "Mrs. Anderson explained everything to me, and it all made sense. Now I have that peace and joy you were telling me about Rebecca."

"That's awesome, Loretta! Now, we're sisters in Christ!" Rebecca said. She got up and hugged her friend.

"I'm so happy for you, Loretta," Scott said. "I've given the matter some thought, and here's what I *can* do for you if you wish. I'll take you to the Whatcom County Pregnancy Center in Bellingham on Monday after school, to get examined and to get some counseling. Then, if you're pregnant, Rebecca and I will go with you to meet with your parents, and with Butch and his father to tell them the news. If it proves true that your parents won't support you, we will work something out so you can carry the child to term. Whether you choose to keep the baby or put it up for adoption, I'll support you, but I can have nothing to do with any decision to abort the baby. What would you like to do?"

"I'll go with you on Monday to see a doctor. Then I can decide what to do from there."

"Let me pray for you, Loretta," Rebecca said. "Dear Heavenly Father, please be with Loretta and give her wisdom to know what to do. And help her parents to have grace. Please give her courage to face the future. In Jesus's name, amen."

"Thanks. I've never heard anyone pray for me like that. It's like you know God personally. That's like so cool."

"Now that you have a personal relationship with God, you can pray that way too," Scott said. "Just talk to Him like He was right here with you every day. And you should read your Bible, too."

"Okay, I have the Bible my grandma gave me. So I just talk to God like I'm talking to you? I don't have to confess to a priest or anything?"

"That's right, honey," Mrs. Anderson said. "You have a direct line to Heaven now. You should confess your sins directly to God. Just share with Him whatever is on your heart, dear."

"You should come to church with me tomorrow," Rebecca said. "You'll enjoy it a lot more than the services at St. Paul's."

"I don't think my parents will allow that," Loretta said. "I can ask them, but I wouldn't bet on it."

"Okay, send me a text if they say you can go, and we'll go together," Rebecca said.

"I'd better get home," Loretta said. "I still have to do my Saturday chores. Thanks so much for everything, guys."

Mrs. Anderson hugged the girls, and Rebecca and Loretta drove back to the Robinson house.

"What happened with you and Scott?"

"We broke up for now. We're going to take a break and see what we really want to do. We're still friends and still going to Paris together."

"Well, I sure hope you two work things out because I think you're perfect together."

Both girls walked across the street to the Flannigan home to do Loretta's chores and Rebecca encouraged her to start with the Gospel of John for her daily Bible reading. Loretta pleaded with her parents to let her go with Rebecca to church the next morning. They reluctantly relented.

When Rebecca returned home, she promptly went up to her bedroom, closed the door, and cried on her bed. Her mother came into her room to see what was going on.

"Rebecca, what's wrong?" Mrs. Robinson asked.

"Scott and I broke up."

"Oh no, that's awful. What happened?" Mrs. Robinson came over and held her daughter.

"I can't tell you, Mom. All I can say is we had a disagreement."

"So I guess we're not going to Paris."

"No, the trip is still on. Scott's family still wants us to come with them."

"But won't that be awkward if you and Scott have to be together for two weeks? If you aren't comfortable being around Scott, we can stay home."

Rebecca leaned on her mother's shoulder and wiped away her tears.

"It's alright, Mom. I still want to go. Perhaps it will give Scott and me time to work things out."

"That would be wonderful! Your father and I really like Scott. We think you two make a great couple—and not just because his family's rich. We've seen how well you interact with each other."

"It sure isn't working very well right now! I guess we don't know each other as much as we thought we did."

"Honey, all couples go through low points. Your father and I have had our share of spats. But you learn and grow from those times. Working through problems helps cement your relationship."

"I hope you're right because I still love Scott even if I'm not very happy with him right now."

"If he feels the same way, then there is still hope for your relationship. You want me to bring a tray up for you, or are you coming down for supper?"

"I think I'd rather eat in my room tonight if you don't mind."

Mrs. Robinson went to prepare their supper and bring Rebecca a tray.

Rebecca spent the evening in her room catching up on her homework. She was thrilled that Loretta now knew the Lord. Rebecca wanted so much for her best friend to have the same joy that she had. She also was concerned about how Loretta's parents would take the news that their daughter was pregnant. That night before she went to bed, Rebecca prayed, "Dear Lord, please help Loretta. Thank you so much for saving my best friend. I know she messed up, but she really needs your help now. Please give her Your wisdom and grace to get through this trial." Rebecca also called out to God, "Lord, my heart is broken. I thought for sure Scott was the one. Now I don't know what to think. Please lead us in the way we should go. Help us to work out our differences if it is your will for us to be together, amen." Rebecca cried herself to sleep that night.

CHAPTER 17

The Revelation

Sunday morning, Loretta showed up at Rebecca's house with a little extra skip in her step. She was wearing one of her best red dresses, a white sweater, and shiny black shoes. Rebecca was wearing a pastel pink dress. Rebecca drove them to Whatcom Community Church in Scott's BMW.

"OMG, I never knew so many people went to this church!" Loretta exclaimed.

"I felt the same way when Scott took me here for the first time," Rebecca said.

Loretta followed Rebecca to her Sunday school class on First Corinthians. When everyone gathered in the main auditorium afterward for the worship service, Loretta just observed everyone.

"That was like totally awesome!" Loretta exclaimed after the service. "I like the pipe organ at St. Paul's, but this church totally rocks! And I wasn't even bored by the preacher."

"I'm glad you enjoyed the service, Loretta. Would you like to go to youth group with me this evening?"

"What's youth group?"

"Oh, you'll love it! Pastor Jake leads this group just for kids our age."

"I'll have to ask my parents. I'll let you know later Rebecca. It should be okay; my dad will be at his pub this evening working, and my mom just watches TV."

Loretta did go with Rebecca to the youth group meeting that evening, and afterward, they went to Rick's for ice cream. They sat in a booth with Scott.

"I had a good talk with my mom this afternoon," Scott said. "She thinks Loretta should break the news to everyone from the comfort of our dining room next Saturday because it's a neutral setting. Does this sound like something you would like to do, Loretta? Depending on how things go tomorrow at the clinic, I can deliver invitations to everyone this week."

"I like that idea. That way I can tell everyone at once and get it over with," Loretta said.

"No matter what happens, you know we're like here for you, girlfriend," Rebecca said.

"Thanks, guys, I couldn't handle this without friends like you. What can you tell me about Sean, Scott? I noticed he was watching me a lot this evening. It looked like he was seriously crushing on me. I think he's kind of cute."

"Sean is a good guy and my best friend, but he has some history," Scott said. "While he was in middle school he got involved with a gang and was arrested for stealing a car. He spent a year in juvenile detention. Then he met the Lord and was able to turn his life around. He's a senior at Bellingham High School, but his family attends Whatcom Community Church. Do you want me to talk to him for you?"

Loretta said, "I'm not sure I'm ready for another boyfriend yet, but I'm open to being friends. I think I need to like take things real slow for now. Is it okay if I go to youth group with you each Sunday, Rebecca? My parents don't mind, but they want me to keep going to St. Paul's in the morning, with them."

"That would be awesome!" Rebecca exclaimed.

"I hate to be a buzzkill, but it's almost ten o'clock ladies, and you have school in the morning," Scott said.

"Yes, Dad!" The girls said in unison and laughed.

They all went home. Rebecca was excited about having her best friend at the meeting.

Monday evening, Loretta sent Rebecca a text confirming that she was indeed pregnant and that her parents had accepted the invitation to the Andersons for dinner Saturday evening. Scott texted Rebecca that the sheriff and Butch were coming, too, so the stage was set for Loretta to share her news.

Saturday evening, Rebecca rode with the Flannigan family to the Anderson's estate. She gave Mr. Flannigan directions, and they parked in the circular driveway in front of the house about the same time Sheriff Brown and Butch showed up.

"Come on in, everyone," Scott said. "Dinner should be ready soon. Make yourselves comfortable in the living room." Scott directed them to the living room, where everyone sat until Mrs. Anderson summoned them to dinner.

"Good evening, you all!" Mrs. Anderson said. "Welcome to our home. My husband Ashley is on a business trip, so he won't be joining us this evening. If you all will come this way and find your seats at the table, we'll get this shindig started."

"You have a lovely home, Mrs. Anderson," Mrs. Flannigan said.

"Your invitation came as quite a surprise to us," Mr. Flannigan said.

"Thank you," Mrs. Anderson said. "And please call me Mary Ann."

"Look, Dad. They have name cards for us at our seats," Butch remarked.

"That's how formal dinner parties are done, Son," Sheriff Brown said.

Mrs. Anderson arranged for herself to be seated at the head of the table with the Flannigans on her left and the Browns on her right. Then she placed Rebecca between Loretta and Scott, who sat at the other end of the table. Butch sat next to Scott.

"Now before we eat, Scott, please ask the Lord's blessing on our meal," Mrs. Anderson said. "And for those of you not familiar with all this hardware, just start at the outside with the salad fork and work your way inside."

After Scott had prayed, Mrs. Anderson rang a little bell by her plate to summon their butler, who began by serving everyone a salad.

"Do you always eat this fancy?" Butch asked Scott.

"No, we wanted things to be special for you tonight," he said. "We usually just eat in the kitchen."

"Hey Red, didn't we like have fun?" Butch remarked with a sly snicker.

"Dude, I've so moved on to something much better," Loretta retorted.

"Oh yeah, and what might that be? Do you have another boyfriend already?"

"You might say that. I've accepted Jesus as my Savior and started going to youth group at Whatcom Community Church. You should try it, Butch."

"You mean *you* of all people have got religion? No thanks, Red!"

"Not religion Butch, but a *relationship* with the only true and living God," Scott said.

"Whatever!" Butch said with a snarl.

The butler brought out some sautéed veggies, followed by Beef Wellington, Shepherd's Pie, and finally, Crème Brûlée for dessert. While everyone was finishing their dessert, Loretta took a big gulp of her sparkling cider, stood up, and tapped her glass to get everyone's attention.

"Everybody, I've like an announcement to make. I'm pregnant, and Butch is the father. I'm so sorry, Mom and Dad. Please don't hate me for this."

Butch sat up straight in his chair as panic covered his face. Both sets of parents looked shocked at first. The fathers turned angry. Mrs. Flannigan began to cry.

"Butch, are you out of your mind? Why didn't you use protection?" Sheriff Brown raised his voice at his son.

"Loretta, how could you do this to us!" Mr. Flannigan said. "How long have you known? How many people know about your pregnancy?"

"Everyone, please calm down!" Mrs. Anderson said.

Butch just sat there in stunned silence throughout the commotion.

"Dad, I got confirmation last Monday at the Whatcom County Pregnancy Center. Besides the clinic, only the people in this room know I'm pregnant. I wanted you all to know since Butch is the father. I'm going to have the baby, and I want to put it up for adoption because I'm too young to raise a child right now. I know it was stupid for Butch and me to hook up. Mom and Dad, please forgive me."

Betty Flannigan got up and held her daughter. Through her tears, she said, "Oh Loretta, of course we forgive you. We're here for you, honey."

"Speak for yourself, Betty!" Mike Flannigan snapped. "Since you plan to have the baby and not get an abortion, you're not welcome in our home again until after the kid is born. You're going to have to go away for a while, so you don't bring shame on our family."

"Mike, do you really mean that?" Mrs. Anderson said. "Don't you love your daughter? Yes, Butch and Loretta made a mistake, but they don't need condemnation right now. Loretta needs compassion from both her parents. Besides, this news will spread fast in a small town such as Whatcom and then what will you do about your precious reputation? Isn't your daughter more important?"

"With all due respect, Mary Ann, this is none of your business," Mr. Flannigan said. "Come on Betty; we're leaving."

"Mike, Mary Ann is right," Mrs. Flannigan said. "Loretta is not going anywhere. And as for you, young lady, we need to talk about what to do with the baby. Thanks for dinner, Mary Ann."

"Mike, if Loretta needs anything or help with medical bills, please let me know," Sheriff Brown said. "Butch will be getting a part time job to help out. It's high time he assumes more responsibility for his actions."

"Thanks, Bud, we'll get back to you on that," Mr. Flannigan said.

Everyone left the Anderson estate and returned home. Mr. Flannigan said he would drop off Betty and Loretta, and then go to his pub to think things over. The two families were in such a rush to leave that Scott had to drive Rebecca home.

As they sat outside the Robinson home in his car, Scott said to Rebecca, "That was quite a ruckus tonight."

"Yes, I thought for sure Mr. Flannigan was going to hurt someone."

"And what about Sheriff Brown? It's a wonder he didn't thrash Butch right there on the spot."

"I feel sorry for Loretta. I'm glad her mom supports her. But it's always been that way. Loretta's father has never cared much for his daughter."

"That's too bad. No wonder she got involved with Butch."

They both sat there in awkward silence for a few minutes.

"Have you guys got your passports yet?"

"Yes, they came yesterday. So when do we leave for Paris?"

"We leave in about three weeks. See you later, Rebecca."

Rebecca went into her house and got ready for bed. She hoped Loretta's dad changed his mind. She would hate to see her friend shipped off to some home for unwed mothers. That seemed awfully cruel and old-fashioned. *It would be great if Loretta and Sean got together. They would be perfect for each other.* But then, Rebecca had known Scott for only a couple months and already they were broken up. She wondered—if they couldn't make their relationship work after that amount of time, what chance did they have? Would going to Paris together really change anything.

CHAPTER 18

The Bad Boy

Loretta went to the youth group meeting for a second time with Rebecca. It was late May. She'd enjoyed it so much the first time, as a new believer, that she was really looking forward to spending time with all these new friends.

A buff young man with short red hair and blue eyes walked up to her. She knew he was Sean, from her earlier conversation with Scott. He said, "Hi Loretta, I'm Sean O'Brian. I'm glad you're coming to youth group. Would you like to go out sometime?"

"You'll have to talk to my father about that," Loretta said. "My parents are not likely to let me date anymore."

"And why is that?"

"Because before I accepted Jesus as my Savior, I like made a huge mistake and hooked up with Butch Brown, the Sheriff's son, and now I'm pregnant." Loretta felt herself blush. "So if you don't want to date me because I'm damaged goods, I'll understand."

"Then that makes two of us, Loretta. Before I came to Christ, I slept around with any girl I could get, and I was only thirteen! I also got in trouble with the law for stealing a car. But that's all in the past. In Christ, we are new creations and can start over almost fresh. I like you Loretta and want to get to know you better. So, I'll talk to your parents. I think if they see that my intentions are honorable, maybe they'll let me go out with you."

"I'd like that. Why don't you come by my house next Sunday after church? My father owns Flannigan's Irish Pub here in town, so the only time you can talk to him is at Sunday dinner. I'll tell my parents to expect you."

After the meeting, as was their practice, everyone went to Rick's Diner for ice cream. Scott, Rebecca, Sean and Loretta all found a booth by the windows.

"I see you two got together. So when are you going on your first date?" Rebecca asked.

"I still have to get her parents' blessing," Sean said. "I'm going over to the Flannigan's home for dinner next Sunday."

"Remember to ask her Dad specifically for permission to court his daughter," Scott said. "If he sees you're sincerely interested in Loretta, he's more apt to trust you."

"Yes, I was planning to do that, and to assure him that I have purposed not to have sex with her or any girl again until I'm married."

"So what else can you tell me about yourself, Sean?" Loretta asked. "Besides being a former bad boy, what's your story?"

"I'm a senior at Bellingham High School. My dad works for the Bellingham Police Department, and my mom sells real estate. Most of our family is in New York, and like your family, ours is of Irish decent. What do you like to do, Loretta?"

"I like to shop and talk a lot," Loretta said. "I also like romantic evenings and picnics. What about you?"

"Oh, I like most sports. Scott and I play basketball with Daniel sometimes."

"Have you seen the latest show at the Bijou? I just love romantic comedies."

"I hate to admit it, but I do, too."

"Yes, that's a real tear-jerker," Rebecca said, and then she turned toward Loretta. "So what's the deal with your pregnancy? Is your dad still going to send you away?"

"No, my mom got in my dad's face and insisted I stay home, and she wants me to keep the baby. She promised to help me care for it, so I don't have to drop out of school. I guess she wants her first grandchild to stick around, which is fine with me. I don't think I could give my baby to strangers. Oh, and Sheriff Brown called and said Butch will be working part time at the police station to earn money to help me with doctor bills and stuff."

"That's great! I would be totally bummed if you had to go away," Rebecca said.

"Yes, I'm happy things are working out for you, Loretta," Scott said. "Pastor Jake's lesson tonight was pretty sobering and scary. But I'm glad he warned us about the dangers of pornography and human trafficking. It's good to know the tricks those rascals use to deceive young women into thinking they have a great boyfriend only to get sold into prostitution—or worse. He needs to take this message to all our schools. If some guy tried to do that to any of you ladies, I would be in prison because he wouldn't live to tell about it. I think it's despicable what these people do to innocent young girls and boys."

"I hear you, bro," Sean said. "I would be right there in jail with you."

"I didn't tell you this Scott, but when I saw your room, I really appreciated that you don't have any 'girlie' pictures on your walls," Rebecca said.

"Thanks. I want to stay pure and save myself completely for my future wife, and I can't do that if I get hooked on pornography. It can really mess a guy up. And I appreciate that you dress modestly, Rebecca. It's hard for a guy to keep pure thoughts if a girl dresses like a prostitute."

"Whoa, I wish somebody told me about this stuff years ago," Loretta said. "I guess I need to reevaluate my clothing choices."

"You would look beautiful to me even in a sweatshirt and jeans," Sean said. "But Scott's right. It helps when girls dress modestly. I've enjoyed this time together, but I'd better get going since I have school tomorrow. Can I give you a ride home, Loretta?"

"Do you mind, Rebecca?"

"Not at all."

They all left together, but Loretta rode with Sean. He followed Rebecca to the girls' respective homes. Loretta gave Sean a peck on the cheek, said goodnight, and scampered up the walkway to her house.

Monday after school, Butch showed up on Loretta's doorstep.

"Hey Loretta, my dad insisted I come over and give this money to you." Butch handed an envelope to her. "I hope you're happy, Red! My dad chewed me out good. Why didn't you just get an abortion?"

"Thanks for the money, Butch," Loretta said. "I decided to keep the baby because I'm not about to kill my own kid! You're welcome to be a part of this child's life, but I'm keeping this baby."

"And what if I want the kid?"

"Butch, do you really want this child? A moment ago you scolded me for not aborting it. I'm willing to work with you to let you visit the child, but he or she is staying in my custody. I'll hire a lawyer to keep custody of this child. Don't mess with an Irish woman. You'll lose every time!"

"Alright, alright you win Red. We don't have to make a federal case of this. You're right; I don't want to be saddled with a kid right now. I'm thinking of joining the Marines after I graduate next year."

"I think the military would be good for you, Butch. Please keep in touch if you're serious about being a part of this child's life."

"Okay, Red. See ya." Butch walked back to his truck and drove away. Loretta was relieved that he didn't want to take legal action. The last thing she wanted was a long, drawn-out custody fight.

Loretta managed to convince her parents to let Sean come for Sunday dinner so that they could meet him. They were very reluctant, however, to let her go out with him. On Sunday after church, Sean was waiting in front of their house in his red Toyota Corolla as the Flannigans returned home from services at St. Paul's Episcopal Church.

"Hello, Mr. and Mrs. Flannigan! I'm Sean O'Brian." He extended his hand to them.

Mr. Flannigan shook his hand and said, "Welcome to our home young man. Come on in."

After they had entered the house, Mrs. Flannigan said, "Sean, please make yourself at home while Loretta and I get dinner ready."

"Are you sure there isn't something I can do to help?" Sean asked.

"Thanks, Sean, but no. Just wait in the living room with Mike," Mrs. Flannigan said.

Sean sat nervously on the couch, and Mr. Flannigan flopped into his favorite chair.

"Since your name is O'Brian, does that mean you're Irish?" Mr. Flannigan asked.

"Yes, my great, great grandfather brought his family over to New York during the Irish potato famine. Most of my family lives in New York."

Loretta carefully listened to their conversation while she set the dinner table.

"You met Loretta at your church youth group. Does that mean you're Protestant?"

"Not exactly; most of my family are Catholic but when my dad met my mom she led him to Christ as his personal Savior, and they started going to her Baptist church in New York. Because you attend church at St. Paul's, does that mean *you're* Protestant?"

"No, we're Catholic, but St. Paul's is the closest thing in Whatcom. Why did you move out here to the Pacific Northwest from New York?"

"I won't lie to you, sir. When I was twelve, I got involved with a gang in New York. Even though both my parents are Christians, and my dad worked for the NYPD, I got in trouble with the law. After I got out of juvenile detention, my dad found a job with the Bellingham Police Department and moved us out here for a fresh start. Then we started going to Whatcom Community Church. I'm living proof of the power of God's forgiveness."

"I'm pleased that you're a God-fearing young man."

"Okay everyone, dinner is ready!" Mrs. Flannigan called out.

They all sat down at the dining room table, which was loaded with meatloaf, mashed potatoes and gravy, green beans and coleslaw. Mr. and Mrs. Flannigan sat at each end of the table, and Loretta and Sean sat across from each other on the sides. Sean had a helping of everything.

"Do you like sports, Sean?" Mr. Flannigan asked.

"Oh yeah, I love sports. I always watch the northwest teams, but I have a New York bias. I also go out for the football, basketball and baseball teams at Bellingham High. Yum! I love your meatloaf. You ladies did a good job. Thanks for letting me crash your Sunday dinner."

"You're welcome, Sean. Can we tempt you with some cherry pie and ice cream for dessert?" Mrs. Flannigan asked.

"Yes, please! I'm so into any kind of pie, especially with ice cream."

Mrs. Flannigan and Loretta cleared their plates and went into the kitchen to dish up the pie and ice cream. They tried to listen in on the conversation between Sean and Mr. Flannigan.

Sean swallowed hard and said, "Mr. Flannigan, I think you know why I'm here. I'd like your permission to court Loretta. Not only is she beautiful but I appreciate her honest and spunky disposition. I really want to get to know her better. I assure you in spite of my past; I have the utmost respect for her. And you should know that I'm committed to not having sex again with any girl until I get married. As for her pregnancy, it's not an issue with me. I still like Loretta and want to see if we're compatible."

"Sean, when Loretta asked us to let you come over for dinner I admit that I wasn't going to let you go out with her since she got pregnant with her last boyfriend. But now that I've met you and know you a little better, I've changed my mind. You have my permission to 'court' Loretta, as you say. You seem like the kind of guy I want my daughter to be involved with, unlike Butch, who is nothing but an irresponsible player and a bully. Of course, your Irish background didn't hurt either," Mr. Flannigan said with a wry smile and a wink.

"Thank you, sir. I'll do my best not to let you down. I'd like to take Loretta out next Saturday to my high school prom, and continue to take her with me to our youth group each Sunday if it's alright with you."

"That will be fine. Just make sure she's home by eleven o'clock."

Loretta wanted to jump up and down for joy at this news. Instead, she and her mom came in with pie and ice cream for everyone.

"So—what did we miss?" Loretta asked with a smile as she placed some pie in front of Sean and then took her seat.

Mr. Flannigan gave a look at Sean and then proceeded to string his daughter along saying, "Sean thinks I should let him court you, but I don't know. He's been such a bad boy; are you sure you want to go out with him? And now he's so religious!" Loretta just calmly ate her pie, then her dad quickly said, "But I think he's a great guy and has my permission to date you!"

Loretta leaped out of her chair and gave her dad a hug. "Oh thank you, Dad! You won't regret this!"

"I believe Sean has something to ask you, darlin'."

"That's right. Loretta, would you like to go with me to my senior prom next Saturday?"

"Would I! Yes, yes, yes! And I have just the perfect red dress—that is if I can still fit into it."

"Okay, I'll pick you up at six o'clock next Saturday. And yes, she'll be home by eleven, Mr. Flannigan."

For the rest of the afternoon, they sat in the living room and watched a college basketball game. Loretta could care less about the game. She was just happy to sit next to Sean on the sofa. After the game, it was time for Loretta and Sean to go to their youth group meeting. Mr. and Mrs. Flannigan watched from the window as Sean and Loretta left at the same time Rebecca left from the house across the street.

Later that night, as they all sat in Rick's eating ice cream, Rebecca teased, "I'm like so happy for you two. Of course, you'll have to quit the cheer squad now that you're dating the competition."

"No, I'll just spy on them for the Wolverines," Loretta shot back. "I'm totally jazzed, Sean, to go to prom with you and meet your friends."

"Why, so you can pump them for information to help the Wolverines? What makes you think I'm not spying on you, too?"

"I'm serious Sean. I want to know more about you, including your friends."

"I know I want to learn more about you, too."

Just then, Butch came into the diner, but this time, he kept his distance from them. Instead, he just sat in a booth alone. As they left, Scott told Butch they were praying for him, but Butch just scoffed.

On Saturday, Loretta's mother did her hair. Loretta had no trouble getting into the dress Scott had bought for her what seemed like so long ago. By the time they were finished, Loretta felt that she was an incredible vision of loveliness in her red dress, with her auburn locks done up on her head. She came down the stairs to meet Sean. He was waiting for her in a white tuxedo with a red bowtie and vest.

"Wow! You look gorgeous Loretta!" Sean exclaimed. "This is for you; it's a red rose corsage."

"You don't look so bad yourself, Sean!"

Mrs. Flannigan pinned the corsage on Loretta's dress and then she took the couple's photo. They left for the prom in a white limousine Sean and his friends had hired for the evening. Along the way, they picked up some of his friends.

"Loretta, this is Ken and Tammy, and Frank and Mary. Everybody, this is Loretta. They're part of my lunchtime Bible study at school."

"Hi everybody!" Loretta greeted them with a smile.

"We're so happy to meet you, Loretta," Tammy said. "Sean is like totally gaga over you, and now I see why."

"Yes, you two look great together," Mary said.

"Aye, she's a pretty special lass, even if she's a Wolverine," Sean teased in an Irish accent.

"And you're a great lad, even if you're a Raider," Loretta retorted with her own Irish accent.

The limousine pulled up at a Bellingham pizza restaurant, and everyone paraded out like they were walking the red carpet at a Hollywood movie opening. The hostess pulled together a bunch of tables and sat them together. They ordered three different small pizzas along with a pitcher of soda.

"So—how did you two meet?" Tammy asked.

"Loretta and I met at our church youth group," Sean said. "She's a new believer and just started coming to our meetings."

"Where did you get your dress, Loretta?" Mary asked. "It's beautiful."

"We bought it at Macy's." Loretta really liked Sean's friends. She looked forward to spending more time with them. "Do you all know what you're going to do after you graduate?"

"I believe God wants me to continue in the 'family business' as a Crime Scene Investigator," Sean said. "I'm going to Whatcom Community College next year for an associate degree, and then I'll transfer to Seattle University to get a Bachelor of Criminal Justice degree."

"Imagine that! A bad boy is becoming a cop," Loretta retorted.

"Actually, we're all going to Whatcom Community College next year, and then moving on to other schools once we decide on a major," Ken said.

"I feel God has called me to the ministry so I'll be transferring to Corban University," Frank said. "Do you know yet what the Lord wants you to do for a career, Loretta?"

"No, I'm not sure yet. How do I like find out what God wants? I'm just a junior at Whatcom High, so I haven't really thought about it much. I'd love to be a professional shopper, and my BFF Rebecca has suggested we start a catering service together. I think it's awesome that you're able to have a Bible study at school. Rebecca and I study our Bibles together at lunch, too."

"Loretta, you really do like to talk," Sean said.

"I told you so. I can't help it. I'm just friendly."

"Ask God Loretta to reveal His will to you for your life and He will make plain the path you should take," Frank said. "Often God uses our natural abilities, likes, dislikes, and talents to shape our way. He will use circumstances or different people or His Word to tell you. Above all, you will have unspeakable peace about whatever it is."

"Thanks, Frank. I'll try asking God what He wants me to do."

After they had finished their pizza supper, they left in the limo and arrived at Bellingham High for the eight o'clock prom. Everyone walked into the gymnasium, which had been decorated with plenty of red and white streamers and balloons. Loretta fit right in, wearing her red dress. Sean found them a table while the other guys rounded up some punch and snacks. Frank and Mary remained at the table while the others took turns on the dance floor. During the first slow song, Loretta started to grind with her back up against Sean.

"Please don't do that, Loretta. That's way too sensual for two unmarried people."

"I'm sorry, Sean." Loretta turned around to face him. "I like thought it was expected of me to dance that way since everybody's doing it. I honestly didn't know any better."

"I realize living a holy life as a new believer is all new to you, but you're a child of the King now, Loretta, so you need to act like it. You're precious to God and also to me. I only want the best for you." He bent his six-foot-tall frame down and kissed her on the forehead.

Loretta smiled sweetly, reached up, and kissed Sean on the lips saying, "Where did you come from, you dear man? I don't think I deserve you."

"And I don't deserve you." Sean gave her a tender hug.

At 10:30 p.m. Sean took Loretta home in the limo and left the others at the school to be picked up later. Sean walked her to her front door and kissed her goodnight.

"I had a great time tonight, Sean. Thanks for taking me. See you tomorrow at church."

"I had a great time, too. You're like so worth it. See ya."

After he had left, Loretta went up to her room to text Rebecca.

"It was like so romantic Rebecca! Sean wore a tux and got me a corsage and even rented a limo. I really like him. How did I get so lucky to meet this great guy?"

"I don't think luck had anything to do with it. I believe God worked in your life to bring you two together."

"Sean and his friends talked about something tonight that got me thinking. Have you asked God what He wants you to do for a career?"

"Yes, and I believe God wants me to become a chef. And I still think we ought to start a catering business together."

"I think you're right. Goodnight, I'll see you at youth group tomorrow. We should talk to Pastor Jake about this."

After their youth group meeting the next evening, Rebecca and Loretta met with Pastor Jake and he gave them some tips on how to discern the will of God for their lives.

"Ladies, I suggest you keep asking God for guidance, keep reading your Bible, and keep alert to any circumstances or people in your lives that provide confirmation," Pastor Jake said. "And most of all you should pay close attention to the influence of the Holy Spirit inside you. If you have absolute peace about your decision, then you can safely assume God approves your course of action. But if you have any doubts, then you should back off. God needs people to serve Him in all professions. You can be caterers for Jesus if that's what God wants you to do."

"Thanks, Pastor, we'll talk to God about what He wants us to do," Rebecca said.

For the next few weeks, Rebecca and Loretta studied the will of God in the Bible and prayed about what they should do. Loretta also was very happy to have Sean as her boyfriend. But, because she was pregnant, her parents wouldn't let her go to Paris with Rebecca. *I hope she brings me back a souvenir. At least I can hang out with Sean. I hope Scott and Rebecca get back together; it would be such a shame for their relationship to be over.*

CHAPTER 19

The Paris Trip

On a Friday in early June, a day with a steady drizzle, the Robinsons and Andersons packed up for their trip to Paris. Loretta stopped in to say goodbye to Rebecca before going with Sean to her doctor's appointment. Only a week earlier they had watched Sean graduate from Bellingham High School. At ten o'clock the Andersons drove up in front of the Robinson house with their Rolls-Royce and a white service van.

"Good Morning, Ralph, are you ready to go?" Mr. Anderson asked when Mr. Robinson opened the door.

"Yes, Ashley, here's our luggage. I have all our passports."

"Great, I'll have the guys put your bags in the van. Please join us in the Rolls."

Once their luggage was loaded in the van, the Robinsons and Andersons packed into the car with Daniel driving. Scott and Rebecca sat in the front seat with Daniel, and their parents and

Roger sat in the back seats. Roger continued to complain about going—until he got inside the car. Once they arrived at Bellingham International Airport, Daniel drove up the ramp and into the back of the plane, which had a specially-designed cargo compartment; the service van followed the Rolls. Rebecca observed that the private 787-10 business jet was white with the blue and yellow Anderson Aerospace logo on its tail. Also a yellow stripe ran the length of the airplane with "Anderson Aerospace" on it in blue letters.

Mr. Anderson led everyone up a circular staircase in the middle of the plane, just aft of the main fuel tank, next to the wings to the main cabin. Mr. and Mrs. Anderson sat in front on the left. Scott and Rebecca sat next to each other behind them, and Mr. and Mrs. Robinson sat across the aisle together on the right side. Roger, Daniel, and the crew sat behind all of them. All of the seats were beige, plush luxury fold-flat seats, to make sleeping easier. They were quite comfortable. It was like flying in a recliner chair. Each seat had its own twelve-inch, flat-screen monitor that folded away for storage in the side of the chair, and each chair had headphones. All the control buttons were in an armrest. The rest of the cabin was decorated in teakwood panels and beige carpet. The ceiling retained the standard 787 LED lighting, but with ornate, carved wood panels framing the white ceiling pockets. There were no overhead luggage bins, so the cabin had a lot more headroom and a wide open, airy feel.

Mr. Anderson's cell phone rang. "Hello, what's up Harry?" Mr. Anderson asked. "Oh no, how bad is it? Okay, keep me up to date on his status. I have to go; we're about to take off."

Mr. Anderson walked to the front of the airplane to see if the pilots were ready to go. A few minutes later he returned, accompanied by a woman wearing a royal blue business suit and yellow blouse. She also had a blue and yellow scarf around her neck.

Mr. Anderson took the PA handset and announced, "Everyone, we're almost ready to leave. Just a reminder to keep your seat belts buckled unless you have to leave your seat. You never know when we may encounter turbulence, and I wouldn't want anyone to get hurt. The lavatories are behind you at the back of the plane, and the closest emergency exits are in front of you over the wings. As far as I know, none of you smoke, which is good, because it's not allowed on this plane. In the event of sudden decompression, oxygen masks will come down from a panel in the ceiling above you. Place them over your face and breath normally. If you need anything, just push the yellow call button on your armrest and Candace will help you. We will be eating lunch and dinner in the dining room towards the front of the plane. Candace will let you know when it's ready." He cleared his throat and continued.

"Scott, I have some bad news and good news for you. The bad news is my chief test pilot got in a car accident on the way to the airport in California and is in critical condition. The good news, Scott, is you get to fly the AX-77 drone now at the Paris air show. Now, let's pause for a moment of prayer. 'Dear Heavenly Father, we commit our care and safety now to you as we travel to Paris. As be Your will, we trust that you will watch over us and bring us safely to and from our destination; and please be with Tom and his family. Comfort them and heal him from his injuries, in Jesus's name, amen.' Now, be sure your seats are in their full upright position and let's go to Paris!"

During his announcement, Candace performed the customary safety demonstration by pointing to the exits. After he had finished, Mr. Anderson took his seat next to his wife, and Candace took a seat at the back of the cabin with the rest of the staff.

"Okay, folks, we're going out to the runway," the pilot said over the PA system. "We've been cleared for takeoff. We'll be flying over Canada, the Arctic, and the North Atlantic all the way to France, and it will take about seven hours. We anticipate arriving in Paris by 9:00 p.m. local time. Relax, and enjoy the trip."

Rebecca looked out the large 787 windows as the plane taxied toward the runway and waited for final clearance. It wasn't long before the pilot swung the plane out onto the runway, throttled up the engines, and took off. Rebecca could barely hear the engines. They ascended in a northward trajectory, and then the pilot banked the plane to the northeast and continued to ascend. Rebecca gazed out the window at the beautiful snow-capped peaks of the Cascade

Mountains below her. For the next two hours, Scott and Rebecca watched the same movie together on their monitors. Candace brought the adults some champagne and the minors some soda. By one o'clock Pacific time, Candace summoned everyone to come into the dining room at the front of the plane for dinner. They sat at the teakwood table on soft beige chairs and buckled their seat belts. Mr. Anderson gave thanks to God for the food and then summoned the chef to begin serving.

"*Bonjour,* everyone!" The chef said. "I'm Chef Claude Rousseau. Today for your dining pleasure, we've prepared some light French dishes to introduce you to French cuisine. But first, a word of warning. It's customary for the French to eat their main meal in the middle of the day, so we have seven courses for you. Please take your time eating. This is a marathon, not a sprint. For our first course, I have some appetizers: Brie and crackers, crudités, and Coquille Saint-Jacques. *Bon appetit!*"

Everyone sampled the veggies, or crudités, except Roger, but he did eat the cheese and crackers. Rebecca thought the scallops, mushrooms, and Gruyère cheese in the Coquille Saint-Jacques was yummy. Next, Chef Claude brought out some small covered containers with beef consommé in them, and salad and vinaigrette dressing. For the main courses, he served broccoli au gratin, Châteaubriand, potatoes Château, and mini brioche rolls. It all smelled wonderful to Rebecca. The adults received mini bottles of red wine and the minors mini bottles of sparkling cider. Finally, for dessert, Chef Claude gave everyone a small Crème Brûlée .

"It was all delicious Chef Claude, as usual," Mrs. Anderson said.

"*Merci,* Madame Anderson. I understand Mademoiselle Rebecca aspires to be a chef. Would Mademoiselle like to talk with me in the galley after dinner?"

"Yes, please!" Rebecca said. "That would be like awesome to pick your brain."

Chef Claude got a peculiar expression on his face at her statement. "What is this 'pick your brain?' I'm not familiar with this idiom."

"It just means I want to learn about your knowledge," Rebecca said.

Chef Claude smiled.

They all left the table now that they were stuffed with French cuisine. Mr. and Mrs. Robinson, Roger, and Mrs. Anderson returned to their seats in the main cabin. Scott and his dad went into the office next to the dining room to go over their roles in the air show, while Rebecca joined Chef Claude in the large galley at the front of the plane. He motioned for her to join him in one of the crew seats in the galley. They both sat down and buckled the seat belts.

"Everything you prepared for dinner was superb, Chef Claude," Rebecca said. "Do you always cook for the Andersons when they fly on this jet?"

"*Merci*, Mademoiselle Rebecca, I normally oversee the restaurant at Monsieur Anderson's hotel in Paris, but he asked me to cook for you on the trip to Paris to acquaint you with French food. Most of the dishes were prepared beforehand in the restaurant kitchen and then warmed up here in the galley. Of course, great care had to be taken to account for the altitude, so no soufflés."

"And no escargot or Foie gras either, I take it, so no one gets grossed out."

"*Mais oui!*" He laughed. "We cannot have people vomiting all over this beautiful aero plane. You are the girlfriend then of Monsieur Scott, *oui*? He is very fortunate to have such a charming young lady in his life."

"Actually, Scott and I are just friends right now, but maybe things will change in Paris. So what advice can you give me to help me become a chef?"

"To start, you must visit Le Cordon Bleu in Paris. Here is my business card. If you have any questions after you start your training, please call me. I would be happy to be a mentor to you, Rebecca."

"Thanks, Chef Claude, I'd like that. I plan to go to Le Cordon Bleu in Seattle. Now, I'd better get back to take a nap." Rebecca walked back to her seat to find everyone stretched out, sleeping. She crawled into her seat, buckled up, and lowered the seat to sleep.

"Did you have a good talk with Chef Claude?" Scott whispered.

"Yes, he wants to be my mentor. What did you and your dad talk about?"

"We just went over the air show schedule. I don't have to fly the AX-77 until Tuesday, so Monday I can take you all sightseeing. What do you want to see first?"

"Awesome! I want to see the Eiffel Tower and Le Cordon Bleu. And I want to do lots of shopping."

"Good, but I think we should consult your parents and Roger as well, to see what they wish to do."

They slept until they were awakened by Candace on the PA system saying, "I'm sorry to disturb you folks, but we're about two hours out from landing in Paris. Chef Claude has prepared some supper for you in the dining room if you're hungry."

Everyone roused themselves and sat down in the dining room again. Chef Claude had placed a large tray of fruit and cheese in the middle of the table. This time, he brought out small dishes of Quiche Lorraine and some crepes with chocolate mousse inside them. Once again, Mr. Anderson gave thanks for the food, and then promptly dug into his quiche.

"Who says real men don't eat quiche? Those who say that just don't know how good it is," Mr. Anderson teased. "After we arrive, we'll need to go through French customs, but then we can go directly to our hotel suite. I won't be able to spend much time with you during the air show, but afterward, I thought we could take some excursions to the Normandy memorial and to the Loire Valley, to see the châteaux. I'll have Daniel drive you around Paris wherever you wish to go. Do you know what you want to do?"

"I'd like to take a river cruise and visit the Louvre museum," Mr. Robinson said. "And yes, this quiche is delicious. I can see us having it for breakfast after we get back," he turned to his wife. "Hint, hint. All the food so far is wonderful. It's a wonder the French don't get fat eating this way."

"I want to see Notre Dame, the Eiffel Tower, and go shopping," Mrs. Robinson said.

"What about you, Roger? Is there anything you wish to do in Paris?" Scott asked.

"Do we get to go to the air show?" Roger asked. "Otherwise, whatever you guys want to do is fine."

"My personal assistant Harry has VIP credentials for all of you for the air show," Mr. Anderson said. "I thought we could all go on Tuesday since Scott has to participate in the demonstration flight of the AX-77 drone. The crowds won't be as thick as they will be on the general public days later in the week, and you can see more that they aren't allowed to see."

"I think you'll like the Louvre, too Roger; they have some cool stuff in there," Scott said.

As they were finishing up their meal, the pilot came on the PA and said, "Folks we're about to start our descent into France. Please return to your seats and make sure they're in the full upright position. We should be landing at Le Bourget within the hour."

Scott and Rebecca gazed out the window into the darkness below, which was dotted with lights. They soon reached the outskirts of Paris, and then the whole ground below them was full of lights, like a bejeweled crown stretching out as far as they could see. As they descended further, Rebecca saw the tops of buildings, and cars moving around on the roads. She even caught a glimpse of the Eiffel Tower in the distance. Soon, they were touching down on the main runway. Rebecca couldn't believe it; they were in Paris!

The pilot taxied the plane to the area where business jets parked. As Daniel and the crew lowered the ramp in back and prepared the vehicles; a car drove up with French customs officials. The officials walked up the ramp and began the process of inspecting everyone's luggage and passports. Once the customs inspection was complete, Daniel and the staff loaded up the van once more, with everyone's luggage. Everyone got into two vans and the Rolls-Royce for the short drive to the hotel north of Le Bourget. They pulled up in front of the hotel like they were the entourage of a celebrity. The hotel staff quickly helped the crew unload the vans and placed everyone's luggage onto several carts, which were then whisked away to the freight elevator to be deposited in their respective rooms on the top floor. The airplane crew followed them. Chef Claude bid everyone goodbye, and went to the restaurant kitchen. Daniel and the other drivers left to park the vehicles in the private parking garage before going up to their rooms, also on the top floor.

"*Bonsoir*, Monsieur Anderson!" the hotel manager said. "We have your suite ready for your party. Please follow me."

"*Merci*, Philippe," Mr. Anderson said. "We're looking forward to a good night's sleep in a comfortable bed."

They followed Philippe to the VIP express elevator and took it to the top floor. Philippe opened the door to a large hotel suite on one end of the floor and handed some key cards to Mr. Anderson. Rebecca was amazed. Beyond the door was a spacious central room with sofas and chairs, and a dining table with fresh flowers on it. Next to the table, double doors opened to a balcony. Off to the left and right were four doors to the bedrooms. The entire suite was decorated in a traditional French provincial style with elaborate white decorative panels on the walls and lush blue velvet drapes. A large, blue oriental carpet covered the hardwood floor. Mr. and Mrs. Anderson took one of the bedrooms to the left and directed Mr. and Mrs. Robinson to take the room next to theirs. Rebecca had a room by herself on the right, and next to her Scott and Roger shared a bedroom.

Mr. Anderson's personal assistant, Harry, came to the suite to deliver their air show credentials and to brief Mr. Anderson on his schedule. Roger went to bed immediately, but Scott and Rebecca stood out on the balcony to take in the view. In the distance, she could see the airport and all of Paris spread out before them like a glittering blanket. After a while, they went to their rooms for some much-needed sleep. Before she went to sleep, Rebecca texted Loretta.

"We arrived safely, Loretta. OMG Paris is breathtaking at night! Our hotel suite is to die for!"

"I wish I was there, Rebecca. I'm still having morning sickness. I'm falling hard for Sean! He's such a dear man. He spends every minute he can with me when he's not working part time at a grocery store, stocking shelves."

"Hang in there, BFF. I need to go to bed. I'll text you later when I get a chance. Good night."

On Saturday morning, the hotel staff brought up a cart with their breakfast on it. Chef Claude had made sure there were fresh croissants, fruit, cheeses, some crepes filled with diced ham and scrambled eggs, milk, coffee, and freshly squeezed orange juice available for them when they awoke.

"Did you sleep okay, Rebecca?" Scott asked as she emerged from her room in her pink bathrobe, pajamas, and slippers. He was already dressed, sitting at the table, reading his Bible and eating his breakfast.

"Yes, oh that's right you're an early riser; this suite is wonderful. I could get used to being pampered like this. What's for breakfast?"

"More yummy stuff from Chef Claude. By the way, did you know that Roger snores?"

"So do you!" Roger said in his defense as he shuffled to the table in his pajamas.

"Good morning, everyone!" Mr. Anderson came out of his bedroom, fully dressed in casual clothes. "Since my schedule is open today, I've arranged for us to take a private river cruise to give you an overview of Paris. We should have time to visit the Eiffel Tower because it's right next to the landing for the cruise boats."

"Awesome!" Rebecca and Roger said in unison.

Mr. and Mrs. Robinson came out of their room to join the party, along with Mrs. Anderson. When they had all finished their breakfasts and were dressed, Mr. Anderson called Daniel to get the car. Ten minutes later, they walked out the main entrance to find Daniel waiting for them. He drove them to the Bateaux Parisiens landing next to the Eiffel Tower, and they boarded the classic motor yacht, Bretagne. All of the Anderson Aerospace staff in Paris for the air show were on board for a pre-air show luncheon and party. For the next two hours, they cruised up and down the Seine River, passing many famous Paris sites such as Notre Dame Cathedral, and the Louvre museum.

"Ashley, do you treat all your employees this well?" Mr. Robinson asked.

"Yes, I try," Mr. Anderson said. "We'll all be working very hard this week meeting with customers and the press, so I reserved all of the top two floors of my hotel for them, and arranged this party. Some have never been to Paris, so I want them to enjoy this experience as much as possible."

"I want you to know Elaine and I really appreciate you letting us tag along like this. It's been a long time since we took a family vacation. And, of course, Rebecca is ecstatic."

Scott and Rebecca went to the stern of the yacht to watch the buildings, people, and other boats go by. Rebecca soaked in the dull roar of the yacht's engine as it churned up the water, as well as the many city sounds all around them. Cars honked, and music flowed from some of the buildings. The smell of fresh bread wafted toward them when they passed a bakery. They had fun waving at people as they passed under bridges.

"This is like so cool, Scott," Rebecca said. "I could never have dreamed of being here in Paris of all places. It's such a beautiful city. And like so romantic."

"I'm glad you're enjoying yourself. And just think—the best is yet to come."

"You'd better tell your friend Sean to watch out. Loretta's falling in love with him."

"That's good. They deserve to be happy. How is Loretta doing during her pregnancy?"

"Not so well. She still has nausea and wishes she could have come with us."

"Monsieur Scott!" An attractive brunette called out in a distinctive French accent. "I heard you were coming. How are you doing?"

"Oh, *bonjour*, Monique! Rebecca, this is Monique; she's my dad's sales rep for Europe. Monique, this is my friend Rebecca."

"It is a pleasure to meet you, Rebecca. *Au revoir,* Scott, I can't wait to see your demonstration of the AX-77 Tuesday."

"You have one in every port don't you," Rebecca teased as Monique walked away.

"I can't help it if girls like me. It's not like I go out of my way to get their attention."

When the cruise concluded, they walked to the nearby Eiffel Tower and rode the elevator to the top. Rebecca walked around the observation deck, taking photos of the city below. A warm breeze constantly whipped her hair around. When they finished, they walked around the gardens below in the Champs de Mars, taking more photos. Later, Daniel drove them to Notre Dame where they toured the cathedral. Rebecca greatly admired the stained glass rose window. Mrs. Robinson lit a candle and prayed in the front of the church. By late afternoon, they were ready to go back to the hotel for some supper and to relax.

That evening, they ate in the hotel restaurant in a private banquet room. Daniel and some of the other staff ate at nearby tables. Chef Claude had prepared a buffet with many wonderful French dishes, including some mini soufflés. When he'd heard that the Andersons and their guests had arrived, he came out to greet them, and placed a small tray with a stainless steel domed cover in front of Rebecca. There was a sticky note attached to the cover that read:

"I hope this doesn't gross you out, but I thought you might want to try these now that you're back on the ground. Chef Claude."

Rebecca laughed out loud when she read the note and opened the cover to find a small plate with some snails and goose liver on it.

"It's a private joke between Chef Claude and me," she said. "I like teased him on the plane about not serving escargot and Foie gras, so he brought some to me." Rebecca tried one of the snails dipped in melted butter. "Mmmm, slimy but delicious; the goose liver isn't bad either. You guys want to try some?"

"I'll take your word for it, Sis." Roger turned his nose up at the dish.

"I'll give them a try," Mr. Robinson said. His wife looked away in disgust as he downed one of the snails. "Surprisingly, it's not bad. I don't think I want a steady diet of these, though."

Scot and Rebecca finished the rest. After supper, everyone returned to their suite to relax before retiring to their respective bedrooms for the night.

On Sunday, everyone stuck around the hotel and relaxed at the spa. Before going to bed that night, Scott made a plea to everyone regarding their site-seeing Monday.

"Everyone, please try to get up early so we can get a good start on the day," Scott said.

"That would be a good idea since I've asked the hotel's concierge to arrange a private, guided tour of the Louvre for you tomorrow," Mr. Anderson said. "It will take you most of the day to see everything."

Rebecca praised God as she lay in her comfy bed that she was able to finally visit Paris. *I can't wait to see more of this wonderful city tomorrow. I'm so glad Scott's family invited us. I wonder what the Louvre will be like?*

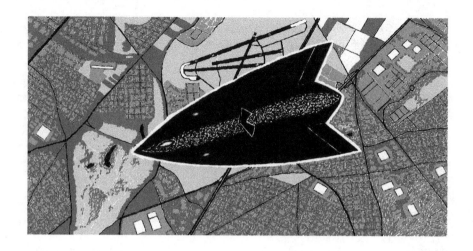

CHAPTER 20

The Air Show

By the time Rebecca came out of her bedroom for breakfast at 7:00 a.m. on Monday, Mr. Anderson was gone. Everyone else quickly got dressed in order to meet Daniel at the hotel's main entrance for their tour of the Louvre. Rebecca noticed that Daniel had brought a book and some lunch with him. He said he knew they would be there for most of the day. During the tour, Roger loved the medieval weapons exhibit and the ancient Egyptian artifacts; Rebecca and her parents were impressed with the many artistic masterpieces, and couldn't get over how small the Mona Lisa was. However, the whole time they were touring the Louvre, Rebecca noticed two large men in black suits lurking nearby them. She assumed they were part of Daniel's security detail. When they finished late in the afternoon, Scott called Daniel to come pick them up by the museum's main entrance.

As they walked toward the car, Rebecca saw Scott looking at two men with dark helmets on a scooter following a middle-aged female, who looked like a tourist, walking on the sidewalk with her purse hanging loosely from her shoulder. Scott gave a signal to Daniel, who was standing by the car, and then he glanced at them, too. Suddenly, the men drove the scooter up on the sidewalk and grabbed the woman's purse.

"*Arrêtez-vous, voleur!*" Scott yelled in French, which Rebecca thought probably meant, "Stop thief!" Scott's voice distracted them just long enough for Daniel to knock the men and their scooter down, which caused the thieves to sprawl onto the sidewalk. Before they could get up and run, Scott and Daniel were on top of them, pinning them to the ground. The thieves chattered loudly in French and struggled to get free, but it was no use. Mrs. Anderson recovered the purse and comforted the victim, who cried hysterically. Rebecca, along with the crowd gathered around, watched the spectacle in unbelief. At last two gendarmes pushed their way through the throng and arrested the thieves. They took statements from Scott, Daniel, the victim, Rebecca, and all other witnesses. Rebecca was proud of Scott.

The French press wasted no time picking up the story. They were all very happy to get back to the hotel after all the excitement. By that evening, it was major news how Daniel and Scott took down two notorious thieves who had victimized tourists for years. Hotel security had to block the press from entering the hotel. They decided to eat supper in the suite that evening.

In the morning, Mr. Anderson distributed everyone's credentials for the air show; the credentials were on lanyards, which they placed around their necks. Then Daniel drove them over to Le Bourget. Rebecca saw a black SUV following them in one of the Rolls' outside mirrors. Could that be the same people who had given them so much trouble back in Whatcom? While Mr. Anderson met with the press, Scott escorted everyone around the exhibits. Rebecca enjoyed seeing all the different aircraft on display, but the noise of the fighter planes flying overhead was unsettling. After lunch, Scott left them in the VIP section of the grandstand for the flying demonstrations. He went off to the secure hanger of the AX-77 to get ready. Mr. and Mrs. Anderson were with a bunch of generals down in front seated in the tent off to the side. Rebecca watched technicians set up a radar screen in front of the generals and then place facsimile targets out in the field by the tarmac. There was an anti-aircraft missile battery, a tank, a remote controlled jeep with mannequins driving around the field in a circle, and a fuel truck. A French fighter plane finished its demonstration and landed while Scott taxied the AX-77 out in front of the grandstand and stopped it by the tent.

"Ladies and gentlemen, I present to you the AX-77 UCAV," Mr. Anderson said over the PA. He then repeated his introduction in French. "Today, we're going to show you what this aircraft can do. My son Scott is at the controls in its secure hanger. You are about to witness the future of warfare."

He invited all the VIPs to examine the drone up close before the flight demonstration. Rebecca and the generals all walked around the drone. It was only about thirty feet long with a twenty-five-foot wing span and about six feet high. It looked like a large, pointed, triangular wing with hidden engine inlets and exhausts resting on the small landing gear, similar to the wheels on a boat trailer. The drone was completely black with a camera pod on the top and bottom that conformed to its body. Rebecca and the generals soon returned to their seats.

"Now, we have here some target plates we would like you to place out in the field; place them anywhere you wish," Mr. Anderson said to the generals as the AX-77 moved away towards the runway.

A few of them took him up on his offer and walked out into the field, randomly placing the aluminum sheets with targets painted on them in the grass.

"Please pay attention to the large monitor and the radar screen in front," Mr. Anderson said. "You will notice the AX-77 is barely visible on radar."

Rebecca watched the drone speed down the runway and then quickly shoot straight up into the air. She could hardly hear it, and it was completely invisible on the radar screen. Everyone could hear Scott over the PA as he described what he was doing, but no one could see the drone as it circled Le Bourget's airfields. Through a feed to the large monitor in front of the viewing stand, everyone could see what Scott saw from the aircraft's video camera. They watched as he sized up the targets on the ground. Then they heard Scott say, "Targets acquired; making an attack run."

The AX-77 swooped past, about two hundred feet above the ground, firing two directed energy or laser cannons from the wings. In mere seconds, there were explosions and balls of fire coming from all the targets, including the Jeep, moving around in circles. Before anyone could catch their breath, the drone was gone. Nothing was left in the field but the smoldering remains, which the airport fire department quickly extinguished. Mr. Anderson sent some technicians out to the field to recover the metal targets the generals had placed in the grass. The conversation around them was of amazement, not only at the complete destruction of all the other targets but that the metal plates each had a tiny hole burned through them—dead center—thus setting off a small charge on the bottom of each. When the drone landed and taxied back in front again, everyone rose to their feet and cheered wildly.

"Ladies and gentlemen, I think you can see now what a formidable weapon system the AX-77 is, but we would like to put it to an even greater test if you're willing to risk it," Mr. Anderson said to the generals. "Included with the data we gave you on the AX-77 is a card with the name of your nation on it. If you would be willing to risk a fake attack on one of your air force bases within the next twenty-four hours, place that card into this pouch. I will have my wife draw out one of the cards, and that country will receive a visit from the AX-77, which will drop this canister on the air force base chosen." He held up a small metal canister with a speaker in it that simulated an explosion.

All the generals placed their cards in the pouch. Mrs. Anderson looked away, reached into the cloth pouch and pulled out the card with "United Kingdom" printed on it. Immediately, the British general called to put all their RAF bases on alert.

"General, you can warn your bases, but I assure you they won't even know the AX-77 is coming until this canister is on the ground," Mr. Anderson told the British general. "I'm not a gambler, but if your personnel can detect the drone is there before the canister touches the ground, I'll buy every one of them dinner at the restaurant of their choice. That's how much confidence I have in our product."

The crowd dispersed, and for the rest of the afternoon, Scott sat with Rebecca and Roger watching the other aircraft demonstrations. When the day drew to a close, they all returned to the hotel.

"Dad, is it alright if Rebecca comes with me when I 'attack' the RAF base in the morning?" Scott asked.

"I suppose it would be okay since Rebecca has a VIP credential, but normally she would not be allowed near the AX-77 without a security clearance," Mr. Anderson said. "We had all of you vetted with a background check before issuing the credentials. Of course, you'll need to get up at 2:00 a.m. to pull this off while it's still dark."

"Thanks, Dad. You still want to go with me, Rebecca?"

"Yes, Scott, I'll drag myself out of bed that early to see you fly the drone."

"Not me man. That is way too early to be getting up," Roger remarked.

Daniel drove Scott and Rebecca to Le Bourget early Wednesday morning. There were few cars on the road. They were met at the secure hanger by several soldiers armed with machine guns. When Rebecca entered the hanger, she saw the maintainers preparing the drone for its mission. Scott placed a chair for Rebecca near his control station. Then, he handed two metal canisters to the technicians so that they could load them into the weapons bay of the AX-77. Besides the one his father wanted him to drop on the RAF base, Scott had prepared another one for the British soldiers. Scott supervised the installation of that canister and then sat down at the control station while they fueled the drone. Scott powered up the control station. The technicians opened the hanger door and removed the chocks from the wheels of the drone.

Rebecca heard the low whine of the jet engines as Scott rolled the drone outside and headed for the main runway. All along Rebecca could hear Scott speaking to the tower in French. Rebecca saw the drone turn onto the runway, but everything was a blur as the UCAV shot down the runway and quickly left the ground. Rebecca couldn't see much on the video monitor until Scott leveled off the aircraft. Then she could see Paris glittering below. Scott switched off the transponder and all exterior radio communication so that no one would know where the drone was, and then he banked towards the United Kingdom. Within ten minutes, the AX-77 was over the English Channel. Soon, Rebecca could see the lights of the coastal towns in England. Scott began the drone's descent towards London.

As the aircraft approached London, Scott corrected their course with a heading for Northolt Royal Air Force base on the outskirts of London. Rebecca saw the air base below as Scott circled it, looking for the best place to drop the canister. He settled on a clear area in the midst of what appeared to be barracks. Locking in his target with the drone's computer, Scott began his bombing run with a steep dive. The AX-77 flew low over the air base, and Scott opened the weapons bay door, dropping the first canister.

Soldiers poured out of all the barracks, rushing to the canister on the ground. While the men gathered around the canister, Scott prepared for his next bombing run. This time, he flew the drone as low as possible over the courtyard, popped open the canister in the open weapons bay, and showered the men with raw eggs. He then banked the plane around quickly to record the angry and bewildered looks on their faces with the drone's video camera.

"Perfect!" Scott laughed on the intercom. "Now we have video proof that the Brits have egg on their faces from this attack."

"I can't believe you did that Mr. Goody-two-shoes," Rebecca said. She was shocked by Scott's actions. How could a Christian man treat these guys like this?

"We can't believe it either," the technicians monitoring the flight said. "We're gonna hear about this. Your father won't be too happy either, Scott. It's time to bring the bird home to its nest."

"Oh come on guys. You gotta admit the look on those soldier's faces is funny," Scott said. "It's too bad we can't post any of this video on the internet. Maybe we could like leak a photo to the press."

Scott flew the drone away from the air base towards downtown London, where Rebecca saw the reflection of lights on the Thames River. The Tower Bridge was in the distance. Scott squared up the aircraft with the bridge and caused it to dive towards it. Scott flew the drone through the opening on the bridge just above the road and rapidly ascended. He then banked the plane to a southeast heading for the return trip to Paris.

"What do you think you're doing, Scott?" One of the technicians exclaimed. "Your father is going to kill you, not to mention what the Brits will do to you."

"Haven't you wanted to know what this drone can do?" Scott said.

"Please, Scott. Don't wreck this plane," the technician pleaded. "We're talking about a very expensive prototype here. We could all lose our jobs and even worse; we could go to jail."

"Don't worry Fred; I'll be careful. It's a kick in the pants to fly. The AX-77 is a lot more maneuverable than a plane with a pilot in it. I can do stuff with this aircraft no pilot could handle without passing out."

"Yeah I know. I think I'm gonna be sick," Rebecca said. "I never knew you had such an ornery streak, Scott."

For the next twenty minutes, Scott carefully flew the drone back to France. Everyone calmed down again until the aircraft approached Paris, and then Scott got a mischievous grin on his face.

"Time for some more fun, guys." Scott banked the plane towards the center of Paris.

Scott lined up the drone with the Champs-Élysées and then dove in a tight, parabolic curve towards the Arc de Triomphe. The aircraft shot through the large arch at almost 800 miles per hour. Scott guided the drone back up and banked it southwest, towards the Eiffel Tower. In mere seconds, he flew it through the large arches at the base of the tower and let out a whoop. "Yeehaw!"

By now, it seemed that both the technicians and Rebecca were beside themselves with fear, and sat there in stunned silence. Scott brought the AX-77 up to a proper altitude, switched on the transponder and radio again, and headed for Le Bourget. Once again, Rebecca heard Scott conversing in French with the tower. Soon, the drone landed and was taxiing towards the hanger. Scott spun it around so the maintainers could back it into the hanger, and shut everything down.

"Are you ready for some breakfast, Rebecca?" Scott asked.

"Maybe by the time we get back to the hotel my appetite will have returned, you bad boy. It's a wonder I didn't barf all over the hanger."

All the technicians were shaking their heads and commenting in disbelief at what Scott did as they parked the drone back in its hanger. Scott and Rebecca walked to the car and woke up Daniel. The sun was just starting to come up on the horizon as Daniel drove them back to the hotel. On the way, several police cars passed them going in the opposite direction, towards Le Bourget, with their lights and sirens going. Daniel dropped Scott and Rebecca off at the main entrance.

"You two wait in the lobby until I park the car, and I'll escort you back to your suite," Daniel said. After Daniel had left, Scott headed for the elevator.

"Where are you going, Scott?" Rebecca asked. "Daniel told us to wait for him in the lobby."

"I'm tired and hungry, and I just want to go back to our suite. We should be okay. Come on."

Rebecca reluctantly followed him onto the elevator. Just before the doors closed two large men in black suits entered. It was the same two guys Rebecca had seen at the Louvre! She sensed they were in trouble. Scott casually looked at his watch and pushed a button on it. As soon as the doors closed, the two men grabbed Scott and Rebecca, pulled out syringes, and injected each of them in their necks.

The last thing Rebecca saw was the elevator door . . . and then blackness.

CHAPTER 21

The Jail Bird

When she woke up, Rebecca found herself bound to a chair and gagged in a hotel bedroom. Scott was bound to a chair beside her. Rebecca was terrified, and her heart began to race. How long had she been out? She could see daylight through the window, but what day was it? Was it still Wednesday? What were these guys going to do to them? Besides being scared out of her mind, Rebecca was furious with Scott. She wanted so badly to rebuke Scott for getting them into this mess. How could he be so stupid and inconsiderate? If only he had obeyed Daniel, they'd be back in their nice, warm beds instead of being stuck on these hard chairs, starving. Men were talking to someone in the other room. It sounded like they were speaking Chinese.

After a while, Rebecca watched as two policemen carefully lowered themselves down to the balcony outside the bedroom, and then silently opened the balcony doors. Motioning for Scott and

Rebecca to keep quiet, the rescuers cut them both free and then removed their gags.

"Get down behind the bed and keep quiet until we come to get you," one of the policemen whispered. Scott and Rebecca complied. Rebecca violently shook as Scott held her in his arms. The police then raised their guns towards the bedroom door and signaled the rest of the team to enter the hotel room. Rebecca heard a loud commotion in the other room as the police rushed in and arrested the kidnappers. The two policemen in the bedroom told Scott and Rebecca to come with them. They escorted them back to their hotel suite where Rebecca fell into the arms of her parents, crying.

"Thank you, officers, for getting our children back from those kidnappers. It's incredible the lengths the Chinese will go to get the plans for the AX-77," Mr. Anderson said. "It's a good thing Scott has a GPS tracker in his watch."

"You are most welcome, Monsieur Anderson," Captain Jacque Navarre said. "And now, young man, I have a few questions for you. Early this morning we received this photograph of a drone flying through the Arc de Triomphe, and later this one of the same drone flying under the Eiffel Tower. Are you the one responsible for this?"

"Yes, sir. I thought it would be fun and a good demonstration of what the AX-77 can do," Scott said.

"Scott, are you out of your mind?" Mr. Anderson yelled. "Do you realize if anything had gone wrong with the drone you not only would have wrecked a multimillion dollar piece of military equipment, but you could have killed innocent bystanders? Not to mention who knows how many regulations you've broken and the exposure of a classified weapons system to the public."

"I'm sorry, Dad. Now that you put it that way, I understand it was a really stupid thing to do."

"Scott, given your statement, I have no choice but to place you under arrest," Captain Jacque said. "Even though you're underage, the prosecutor may charge you as an adult for this. Monsieur Anderson, you may check with the magistrate later today about the charges and any bail required. I must ask you to surrender your passport, Scott, and come with me."

All the Robinsons watched in shock as the police led Scott away in handcuffs. Mrs. Anderson slumped onto the sofa, sobbing while her husband called his lawyer. The lawyer put them in touch with an attorney in Paris. Rebecca was scared for Scott. Would their trip be cut short because Scott was in jail? Later that day, they watched as Scott was taken before three judges in the Criminal Court to be charged.

"Scott Anderson, how do you plead to these charges?" the senior justice asked.

"Your Honors, I plead guilty and appeal to you to have mercy on me since this is my first offense, and I am still a juvenile. However, whatever punishment you feel is appropriate I will not contest it."

The judges then whispered among themselves for a few minutes, and the chief judge conveyed their decision.

"Scott Anderson, since you pleaded guilty, it is the decision of this court that you pay a fine of 10,000 Euros, have your pilot's license suspended for a year, and you must make a public apology to the French people. Ordinarily, we would have sent you to prison for two years, but because of your help in catching those thieves this week, and your age, we decided to have mercy on you. Let this be a lesson to you, young man. If you stay out of trouble for the next five years, this will not go on your permanent record. You are free to go."

"Thank you, Your Honors."

His parents and Rebecca all embraced him as he walked out of the courtroom. Scott paid his fine, and his dad made arrangements for a press conference at the air show.

"You realize now that you're literally grounded for the next year," Mr. Anderson said. "No more flying for you kid, and no more flying the AX-77 ever again. Your security clearance has been revoked. I'm very disappointed with you, Scott, but your mother and I are relieved you're not going to prison for this stunt."

They went back to the hotel to allow Scott to change his clothes and prepare for the press conference. Then Daniel drove them to Le Bourget, where Scott stood up in front of the press and said in French, "People of Paris and France, and I might add London too, I'm truly sorry for placing you in danger and your beloved monuments in danger with my actions earlier this morning. It was never my intention to show any disrespect to the French or British people. Please forgive me."

Mr. Anderson fielded a few questions from the press, but would not allow them to ask Scott any questions. When he returned to the hotel, Scott collapsed in his bed and slept for a few hours while Mrs. Anderson had Daniel take her, Mrs. Robinson, and Rebecca shopping. Mr. Robinson and Roger remained at the air show. When everyone returned to the hotel that evening, all the ladies showed off their new treasures. Scott took Rebecca aside on the balcony to talk with her.

"Rebecca, I'm glad you got a chance to get some 'retail therapy' today. I should have listened to you and waited for Daniel in the lobby. Because of my carelessness, I put both our lives in danger. Can you forgive me?"

"Yes, I forgive you. Just don't let it happen again!" She teased, whapping him on the arm. "I was scared to death. I thought for sure we were done for. I also was very angry with you for not obeying Daniel. But I'm glad you're not going to prison. I still can't believe you acted so foolishly. It's not like you, or at least not like the man I've grown to love and respect."

"You're right, of course. I gave in to a moment of weakness and set a very poor example for you and the rest of the world. It was very un-Christ-like of me. Still, I have to admit it really was a whole lot of fun. But I've learned my lesson. I promise not to pull a stunt like that ever again."

"Good, because I don't want to bake you a cake with a file in it or visit you in the slammer, you bad boy."

"So you said the L-word. Do you really love me? I love you too, Princess. I could never forgive myself if something happened to you because of my stupidity."

"Yes, I really love you. Apart from recent events, I think you're the most wonderful guy I've ever met. So what are we going to do about it?"

"Honestly, Princess I want to try again. I've been miserable these last few weeks. I've done a lot of soul-searching and seeking God's will about our relationship. I should have been more understanding. So if you'll have me, I want to be your boyfriend again."

"I've been miserable, too. You broke my heart, Scott. So I don't know if I want to try again. Everyone says we have something special. But if we get back together again, you're going to have to be a lot more patient with me. Remember, I'm still a young Christian. I haven't studied the Bible as much as you. I also hope you'll be a lot less judgmental. Don't be a Pharisee, Scott! Now—come here and kiss me."

On the balcony, Scott and Rebecca smooched more passionately than usual. It was like all their pent-up desire for each other was compressed into that one kiss.

"I love you so much, Princess."

"I love you too, my Prince."

"What do you say tomorrow we go check out Le Cordon Bleu?"

"Oh! That would be like so awesome!"

They embraced on the balcony and gazed at the city lights for a few more minutes. The warm summer breeze felt wonderful on Rebecca's face, and so did being held once again in Scott's arms. Reluctantly, they went to their separate bedrooms. Rebecca wanted to give Scott another chance but was still afraid to fully commit to their relationship lest she get her heart broken again.

In the morning, when Rebecca appeared for breakfast, Scott told Rebecca that everyone else was gone. She'd heard that Mr. Anderson was wrapping up his role in the air show by supervising the loading of the AX-77 on a military transport to be returned to Edwards Air Force Base. Mrs. Anderson took Mrs. Robinson with her to the hotel's spa to be pampered, and Mr. Robinson and Roger went swimming in the hotel's pool.

After she was ready, Daniel drove Scott and Rebecca to Le Cordon Bleu. They pulled up on a quiet street next to a cream-colored building with bright blue panels in the windows. Scott took Rebecca inside and explained in French that Rebecca wanted a tour. A portly man came to show them around all the kitchens and explain their programs, in English.

"Do you know chef Claude Rousseau?" Rebecca asked. "He offered to be my mentor."

"*Mais oui*, chef Claude is one of our guest instructors. He is well-known here in Paris."

After their tour, Scott asked Daniel to take them to Montmartre to see Sacre-Coeur cathedral and to eat lunch. They found a small café where Scott ordered for them. It wasn't long before some of the people recognized him from the news. Daniel kept a careful eye on things as many people came up to Scott and thanked him for catching the thieves and then said they accepted his apology. When they finished eating, Daniel drove them to the Arc de Triomphe for a closer look.

"Ah, returning to the scene of the crime," Rebecca teased as they walked around the massive arch in the center of a huge traffic circle.

"I just wanted you to see it close up so you can better appreciate the scope of my naughtiness. After all, the drone flew through so fast you barely got a glimpse of this magnificent arch."

They went up to the observation deck on top and looked down at the many streets connecting to the traffic circle like spokes on a giant wheel. Rebecca took more photos, and they went back through the tunnel to the Champs-Élysées, where Daniel had parked the Rolls-Royce. Scott took Rebecca for a short stroll down the street to look at some of the shops, and then they returned to the hotel.

Friday, everyone went to see the Palace of Versailles and its gardens. The Robinsons were all in wonder at the size of the palace. Even after spending most of the day there, it seemed like they barely scratched the surface when it came to seeing everything. No one had any trouble sleeping that night after walking so much all day.

No one wanted to go anywhere Saturday, so with much persuasion, Mr. Robinson joined the others at the hotel spa to get his sore muscles massaged. Even Roger was more than willing to try it.

"Now that you feel more rejuvenated, would you like to take a day trip tomorrow to Normandy?" Mr. Anderson asked everyone at dinner that evening.

"Do we have to?" Roger asked.

"No, you don't have to go, but it would be a good education for you to see where our soldiers stormed the beach on D-Day," Mr. Robinson said. "I'm interested in going, Ashley."

"Me too," Rebecca said. "I think Dad's right, Roger. We need to see this. It will help make our history classes more meaningful."

"I've seen the memorial, so I'll just stay here at the hotel if you don't mind dear," Mrs. Anderson said. "Anyone else is welcome to join me."

"I think I'll take you up on that offer, Mary Ann," Mrs. Robinson said.

"Very well. I'll let Daniel know to expect only four of us unless Roger changes his mind," Mr. Anderson said.

They left the hotel early Sunday morning around eight o'clock. Scott and Rebecca sat up front with Daniel again, and Mr. Anderson, Mr. Robinson, and Roger sat in the back. Rebecca loved seeing the French countryside. But, once again, she caught a glimpse of a black SUV following them in the distance. When they arrived at the Normandy American Cemetery and Memorial, they walked out to the meadow where there was row after row of white grave markers. Tears came to Rebecca's eyes when she saw that so many had given their lives during the invasion. It was overwhelming.

On the way back to Paris, they went to the city of Bayeux to look at the Bayeux Tapestry at the Musée de la Tapisserie. Rebecca was amazed at the 230-foot-long, eleventh century, embroidered tapestry celebrating William the Conqueror's conquest of England in 1066. The sun was starting to set when they arrived at the hotel.

"Before you all go to bed tonight, you should pack everything you can," Mr. Anderson said. "Tomorrow, we're leaving as early as possible for the Loire Valley for a few days before we return home. We won't be coming back here, so don't forget anything."

Rebecca wondered what all the castles in the Loire Valley would be like. She hoped the black SUV she'd seen earlier didn't mean more trouble for them. *Why can't those guys just leave us alone?*

CHAPTER 22

The Loire Valley

By eight o'clock Monday morning they were all packed up, and
their entourage headed out first for Chartres to see the famous
Gothic cathedral. Rebecca listened from the front seat of the Rolls
as Daniel contacted their security "eye in the sky" to confirm their
route was clear of threats along the way. When they drove up to
the cathedral, Daniel told the helicopter pilots they could take a
break for an hour. Rebecca could see why Chartres was considered
one of the finest examples of Gothic architecture.

"I love the stained glass windows here better than those in
Notre Dame!" she exclaimed. "They're like absolutely gorgeous!"

"Yes, I like this church too," Scott said.

From Chartres, they traveled south through Orleans to Château
de Chambord. All the Robinsons were in awe of the magnificent
château.

"Dude, this is like the mother of all castles!" Roger exclaimed.

"I think the turrets and massive circular staircase are so cool," Rebecca said.

"So is this château big enough for you?" Scott teased.

"Maybe for a summer house, but I think Versailles would be a better main house," she said with fake affectation pointing her nose in the air. "My tastes are simple; I only like the best."

"You don't ask for much, do you?"

"But seriously, I don't really need any of this fancy stuff. It's enough for me just to be with you, Scott."

While at Chambord, they ate lunch at the Hotel St. Michel's restaurant, next to the château, before moving on to Cheverny, to the south. From there they went to the city of Blois to wrap up the day. Mr. Anderson secured the entire top floor of the Mercure Hotel for them.

Tuesday morning after breakfast, they began the day with a visit to the Château de Blois. Roger thought the fireplace with the golden "dinosaur" dragon above the mantel was impressive. Rebecca liked the four-poster beds. Then they drove southwest along the Loire River.

"Big Kahuna, this is Eye in the Sky, there are two black SUVs shadowing you on both sides of the river," Craig, the helicopter pilot, said.

"Thanks, Eye," Daniel said. "I think they're waiting for an opportunity to box us in, so we should confront them by the long bridge at Chaumont-sur-Loire. There is less chance of collateral damage to the local population. Pack Mule, you block the bridge until we cross, and Eye, you try to stop the other SUV on the other side so we can get across the bridge."

"Roger, Big Kahuna!" both Craig the pilot and Sam in the luggage van said.

"Oh, oh, we're not alone up here!" Craig exclaimed. "It looks like they have a helicopter, too."

"You're breaking up, Eye," Daniel said. "I think they're trying to jam our radios."

Rebecca looked out the window and saw two helicopters flying over the river. One of them turned sideways and flames shot out from beneath it followed by a loud "pop, pop, pop." The other helicopter quickly left.

"Big Kahuna, we just took out their jamming pod with our fifty cals. Now we're going after the SUV on the other side of the river from you."

"Roger, Eye," Daniel said.

Meanwhile, Daniel drove around the traffic circle by the bridge and then started across the bridge as fast as he could, while Sam and Seth blocked the entrance to the bridge behind them with the luggage van.

Rebecca watched the helicopter dive down to the road on the other side of the river. Again, flames shot from beneath it at a black SUV that was approaching the bridge. She saw someone in the SUV fire back at the helicopter before they stopped abruptly on the road. Rebecca also heard gunfire behind them on the other end of the bridge.

"Big Kahuna and Pack Mule, the French authorities are closing in on the bridge," David, the co-pilot, said. "We took out the other SUV, but Craig got hit, so we're heading off to the nearest hospital."

"Eye, this is Pack Mule," Sam yelled into his radio. "We could use your help before you go. These guys have us pinned down."

"Roger Pack Mule, the cavalry is on the way."

Rebecca watched the helicopter cross the river and dive towards where the van was positioned. Again, flames and noise came from beneath the helicopter. She craned her neck to the back to see what was happening, but her view was blocked.

"Big Kahuna, this is Pack Mule. The bogy is neutralized," Sam said. "We'll deal with the authorities and move on to the hotel. Enjoy the rest of your tour."

"Roger, Pack Mule," Daniel said.

"Mercy! You certainly don't lead a dull life," Mr. Robinson remarked.

"Yes, unfortunately, it's necessary these days to have plenty of security," Mr. Anderson said. "Industrial spies are relentless. I can't tell you how many times they've tried to hack into our computer systems. But we have countermeasures that include offensive cyber-weapons designed to destroy their computers. Some of our IT people have a wicked sense of humor. Apparently, if someone tries to breach our firewall, they're given one warning to cease and desist. If they persist, a dragon graphic appears on their screen and growls, 'You were warned!' before frying their system. Plus, all of our classified and proprietary information is on a separate, isolated computer network. I don't know about you, but I believe we've had enough excitement for one day. I don't think the people behind this will try anything more today."

For the rest of the day, they visited the Chaumont-sur-Loire, Amboise, Chenonceaux, and Azay Le Rideau castles before coming to the outskirts of the city of Tours and La Bourdaisiere hotel/château.

"Awesome!" Rebecca exclaimed. "We get to stay in an actual castle! Like how cool is that?"

"We thought you'd like this," Scott said.

They wasted no time getting settled in their rooms. Sam and the staff already had everyone's bags in their respective rooms. Since they still had about an hour before dinner, Roger and his dad found the swimming pool and Elaine Robinson and Ashley and Mary Ann Anderson relaxed in the living room. Scott and Rebecca went for a walk in the formal gardens. They were followed by Sam, as their bodyguard.

"This is like so romantic," Rebecca said. "If I'm dreaming, nobody wake me up."

"You're not dreaming, Princess. Come on. Let's get a photo of us in front of the château."

"I feel like royalty here. You should see the bed in my room. It's so fancy."

Scott beckoned Sam to take their photo while they posed by the château. They then continued their walk while Sam kept a respectful distance behind them.

"So, do you think our relationship has any hope?" Scott asked.

"I would like to think so, but I'm not sure I want to live in a fishbowl," Rebecca said as she looked over her shoulder at Sam, who stood by a tree, watching them.

"I imagine it's quite unnerving for you, Princess, all this security stuff. But you get used to it." Scott turned towards her and took both her hands.

"That's the thing, I don't know if I want to get used to it. I love you Scott, and I realize if I stay with you it's a package deal. I'm just weighing my options. I know I've never met a guy as wonderful as you. And being with you would ensure I have a future away from Whatcom, financial security, and a whole lot more exciting life if today is any indication. But I'm concerned about our safety. If something happened to you, I would be devastated."

"Princess, our times are in God's hands. Even in Whatcom you could be in danger. Bad stuff happens. You just have to take precautions and trust God with the rest."

"I'm still worried about you becoming a workaholic like your father."

"I promise you, Princess, if I were with you I would never become a workaholic. And if I start to head in that direction, you have my permission to call me on it. I told you I don't want to be anything like my father when it comes to work. I like having fun too much! I want to enjoy my family."

"That's another thing. I want to spend a few years working as a chef before having to deal with children. The way you're talking it sounds like you want to have children right away."

"No, I want to finish my education and get established with my career as an engineer first. I also believe it's healthy for a couple to spend a few years together alone before taking on the responsibility of children. That way, they can work out any kinks in their relationship and enjoy one another before the little munchkins take over their lives." Scott placed his arm around Rebecca's waist and held her close to him and she put her arm around Scott's waist as they continued walking.

"If you don't want to live in Whatcom, Rebecca, where would you want to live? What if I inherit my parents' property there after they die? Would you expect me to sell my family home?

"Scott, I really don't care where I live as long as it's with you. We could live in a shack on the beach for all I care. I just want to explore other places around the world and not get stuck living in Whatcom all my life. When the time comes, we can work out what to do with any inheritance. Perhaps by the time we have children, we would want to live in Whatcom so they could be close to their grandparents."

Scott looked at his watch and turned back towards the château. "I can live with that, Princess. That's one of the things I like about you, Rebecca. You're not what I would call high-maintenance. You don't seem to care a lot about material stuff."

"Hey, I like nice stuff, but it wouldn't be the end of the world if I didn't have it. Rest assured; I'm not some gold digger. I want financial security, but I don't need tons of money to be happy."

"That's good because to start out we wouldn't have as much as my parents have. We would probably be comfortable, somewhere around six figures between the two of us, however."

"This has been a good talk, my Prince. You've given me more hope for us than when we started. I'm getting hungry."

Scott and Rebecca held hands and returned to the hotel for dinner.

All their party ate dinner in a private dining room at a long table with cushy, red velvet chairs. After Mr. Anderson had given thanks for the food, Mr. Robinson proposed a toast, "Here's to the Andersons for hosting this trip. Thank you so much for including our family. This is something we'll never forget, believe me."

"What was your favorite part of our visit to France, Rebecca?" Scott asked.

"Everything! But if I had to pin it down to one thing, it's just sharing this with you, Scott. What about you?"

"The best part of this trip for me was to see you and your family's reactions to the whole experience . . . and flying the AX-77!"

"You're not completely repentant, are you," Rebecca teased.

"Yes and no. It was a lot of fun flying under the Arc de Triomphe and Eiffel Tower, but it really was a stupid thing to do. I guess I made history. Only three other pilots have flown under the Arc successfully. I'm the only one to do it with a jet powered aircraft, and only the second one to fly under the Eiffel Tower. I could have never done it without the drone's computer to calculate the ideal flight path, though. And at that speed, there is no room for error which compounds how incredibly foolish it was to do it."

"Well, I hope you got all of that craziness out of your system. I want you to stick around for a while."

After dinner, everyone hung out in the large living room of the château for a couple of hours before returning to their respective rooms for the night. Rebecca reviewed all the things they had done in France and thanked God for Scott and his family before she fell asleep.

In the morning, they returned to the dining room for breakfast. Rebecca handed her suitcase to Sam so he could put it in the luggage van, and she overheard Daniel notify the helicopter patrol they were ready to head out for Paris. For the next three hours, their entourage had an uneventful journey back to Le Bourget in Paris. When they drove up beside the 787, French customs was waiting for them. Mr. Anderson's security team was just finishing their inspection of the plane with bomb-sniffing dogs along with French Customs' drug dogs. The French officers checked everyone's bags and passports. Then, while Daniel and the staff loaded the bags back into the vans and parked all the vehicles in the cargo compartment, the Robinsons and Andersons climbed the aero stairs beside the main entrance to the cabin. They were greeted by Candace and Lois in the vestibule.

Once Daniel and the other staff were seated, the pilots taxied out to the main runway. Soon they were rushing down the runway and soaring into the sky over Paris. The pilots banked the plane to a northwest heading and continued to climb.

"Goodbye Paris," Rebecca remarked as she held Scott's hand. "It's been fun."

Rebecca and Scott watched a movie until Candace announced that dinner would be served in the dining room. "Ladies and gentlemen, Chef Claude sent some more goodies with us for the return flight. If you would like to join us in the dining room, we will begin our dinner service."

After a leisurely and delectable dinner, Roger went back to his video game and everyone else settled in for a nap. Rebecca gazed out the window at the snowy mountains of Greenland before dozing off.

Soon, she awoke to Candace speaking on the PA. "Ladies and gentlemen. We're about three hours out from Bellingham. Local time will be around 3:00 a.m. when we land, and it's overcast. We have a light supper or breakfast for you in the dining room."

Everyone ate and went back to their seats for the final descent into Bellingham International Airport. After the plane had touched down, the pilots taxied to the Anderson Aerospace hanger and turned the massive 787 so that it could be backed into the hanger. U. S. Customs awaited them. Once the customs inspection was passed, Daniel and the other staff loaded up the luggage back in the vans, taking care to put the Robinson's bags near the back doors for easy access. The two pilots, and the two attendants, Candace and Lois, said goodbye to everyone and left in one of the vans. Finally, everyone climbed into the Rolls and the second van to return to Whatcom.

It was dark still, and a soft drizzle sprayed down upon them as they drove up in front of the Robinson home.

"Later Dude, I got some serious chillaxing to do," Roger said as he left the car, bumped fists with Scott and walked up to his house with his bags.

"I hear you on that," Scott said. Scott got out and helped Rebecca out of the front seat. Immediately, she clung to him.

"I don't want it to end" Rebecca lamented. "I love you so much and have enjoyed being with you every day."

"I'll see you Sunday morning. Your brother is right. You're going to need a few days to recover from jet lag and get acclimated to the

Pacific time zone again." Scott gently took her face in his hands and kissed her. Reluctantly, she took her luggage and trudged up the walkway.

"Thanks again, Ashley, for including us. We'll have to do something like this again sometime," Mr. Robinson said, shaking Mr. Anderson's hand.

"Next time I go to Alaska, I'll let you know Ralph," Mr. Anderson said. "Perhaps you can break away from your store and do some hunting and fishing with us."

"I'd like that," Rebecca's dad said, grabbing his luggage.

Mary Ann and Elaine hugged before Mrs. Robinson joined her husband and children on the front porch of their home. They all waved goodbye to the Andersons.

Rebecca and her family slept away much of the three days after their return from Paris. Loretta wasted no time coming over to see Rebecca once she learned they were back. She was now starting to show a little but tried to be her usual spunky self in spite of the nausea.

"I'm sorry I wasn't able to see you right away, but we've all been totally exhausted after our trip. Are *you* feeling any better?" Rebecca asked.

"Not really. I know I'm doing the right thing having this baby; I just wish I wasn't so miserable doing it. But Sean is such a dear. He's been incredibly supportive. And Butch has come by a few times to check up on me and give me some money for expenses. There may be hope for him yet."

"Scott and I prayed for you every day while we were gone. So do you want to see my photos? We had like the bestest time. Maybe someday you and I can go to Europe."

"That would be awesome! Sean wants to take me to Ireland. I think things are getting very serious with us. I wouldn't be surprised if he asks me to marry him."

"That's wonderful! Scott and I are back together. I told him I love him, and he said he loves me too. But I'm not sure yet if our relationship will last."

"I'm glad you're back together," Loretta said. "Sean and I have been praying for you and Scott. We think it was a shame that you broke up. Now—show me those photos."

Rebecca was happy for her friend. It was good to see Loretta with a good man for a change. She couldn't believe how serious they were, however, after only having met a few weeks earlier. Was it really possible to know you love someone in such a short time? After all, she had only known Scott for three months, and she felt they had a real connection. But was their love real? Did they have the stuff to go the distance? Rebecca wasn't completely convinced.

CHAPTER 23

The Decision

Loretta slept over with Rebecca Saturday night, and Rebecca told her all about Paris and the châteaux and all her adventures. It was a wonder they got any sleep at all! In the morning, Rebecca dragged herself into the shower and dressed for church. Loretta, of course, was sick to her stomach but managed to keep down a little breakfast. When Scott came by to pick up Rebecca, Loretta decided to go with them.

"I thought your parents insisted you go to St. Paul's in the morning, Loretta," Scott said.

"Now that I'm going out with Sean they've changed their minds. I'll text Sean and have him meet us there."

When Sean arrived at Whatcom Community Church, they all sat together. At the end of Pastor Fraser's sermon, the pastor announced there'd be a baptismal service and barbecue picnic at Lake Whatcom Park on the Fourth of July, and that anyone wanting to be obedient in baptism should meet with him afterward. Rebecca and Loretta looked at each other and knew they had to talk to him.

"Pastor Fraser, Loretta and I want to be baptized," Rebecca said. "We've been studying baptism in the Bible and believe it's the right thing for us to do."

"Pastor Jake has told us all about the true purpose of baptism," Loretta said.

"I'd be happy to baptize you, girls. Let's get together this week and talk about it. It sounds like you young ladies fully grasp the importance of your decision. Will your parents be coming?"

"We don't know," Loretta said. "Our parents aren't exactly enthusiastic about the church, but maybe they'll come since it's a picnic at the park. We'll talk to them about it."

That evening after youth group, Rebecca and Loretta arranged to meet Pastor Jake and his wife the following week to talk about their relationships with Scott and Sean.

On Monday, since school was out for the summer, Rebecca applied for a job at Rick's Diner so she could get more work experience and earn some money for her future education.

"Do you have any experience cooking in a restaurant, Rebecca?" Rick asked when he interviewed her.

"I've been volunteering at the mission in Bellingham. Other than that, my only experience has been cooking for my family at home. I'm planning to become a chef."

"Let me make some calls. If everything checks out, I'll let you help me in the kitchen on a part-time, trial basis. If you do a good job, Rebecca, I'll bump up your hours. So, how soon can you start?"

"I can start right away. Would I still be able to work here after school begins again?"

"Yes, I'm sure we can work something out."

Before the day was out, Rick told Rebecca she had the job and to show up at six o'clock the next morning. Rebecca so impressed

Rick with her skills during the week that he put her on full-time for the rest of the summer.

On Friday evening after work, Rebecca and Loretta drove over to Pastor Jake's house.

"Come on in girls," Pastor Jake said. "This is my wife, Martha."

"Welcome to our home, ladies," Martha said. "Take a seat in the living room. Can I get you something to drink?"

"I'd like a soda please," Rebecca said.

"Me too," Loretta said.

Martha went into the kitchen to get some drinks and snacks while Pastor Jake and the girls settled into the living room.

"Now let me get this straight. You ladies want to talk to us about your relationship with your boyfriends, right?" Pastor Jake asked.

"Yes, we want to know how can you tell if someone is 'the one'?" Loretta said.

"That's a good question. I recently had a similar discussion with some other individuals. I'm thinking of developing a Bible study on relationships."

"How did you and your wife know you wanted to get married?" Rebecca asked.

Martha returned with a tray and sat down next to her husband. They looked at each other, and Pastor Jake proceeded to answer the girls' questions.

"Martha and I met at Bible college. We dated off and on for a couple of years before I asked her to marry me. I knew I wanted to marry her because I spent many hours in prayer and God revealed to me that she was 'the one' as you say. I also got to know her very well and liked being with her. So I grew to love her enough to want to spend the rest of my life with her."

"But how did you know you loved her?" Loretta asked.

"Loretta, love is not some hearts and flowers emotional response. Real love is a decision. Yes, there is an emotional element, but essentially it's a decision to seek the very best for someone and to accept them just as they are."

"When I first met Jake," Martha said. "I couldn't stand him. I thought he was very immature. But then as I got to know him better I learned that he had all the qualities I was seeking in a husband. I guess you could say I grew to love him too. Now I can't imagine my life without him. In fact, it hurts something awful whenever he has to go out of town without me, for ministry."

"I guess what Loretta and I are trying to figure out is if we want to marry our boyfriends. We haven't known them for very long. Is it possible to have love at first sight?"

"No, that's infatuation, and it doesn't last," Pastor Jake said. "Real love is like a delicate flower. It takes time to grow. You have to invest time and effort in a relationship to yield the flower of love."

The wheels in Rebecca's head turned. She wondered if maybe she was just infatuated with Scott.

"Ladies, infatuation focuses more on how the object of your affection can make *you* happy. Real love focuses on how you can make him happy. Your concern is more for his needs than your own. Here are some books I want you to read about relationships. If you have any further questions, we can talk some more. I also have an assignment for you. I want you to write down in two columns all the pros and cons about your relationships. I find this exercise helps me to make better decisions."

"Thanks, Pastor Jake," Loretta said.

"Yes, thanks, this has helped me to understand better what Scott and I have," Rebecca said.

There was a great turnout at the park on the Fourth of July; it was a glorious sunny day for a change. Rebecca was excited that she was getting baptized with her best friend, Loretta. She was glad their parents had agreed to come, too. It looked like most of the town of Whatcom was there by Lake Whatcom for the festivities.

Whatcom Community Church had reserved a large area for their picnic and brought about twenty barbecues. The air was full of the aroma of hamburgers and hot dogs cooking. Plus, all the church members brought various salads, desserts, baked beans, veggies and fruit to place on a long buffet table.

The town council and mayor had hired a company to put on a modest fireworks show from a small barge out in the lake. Plenty of people had also brought their own fireworks to set off on the beach. Mr. Flannigan's pub sponsored the beer garden, and Mr. Robinson and other business owners put up the prizes for the various games the townspeople participated in. The Andersons, Robinsons, Flannigans, and O'Brians all sat together at the picnic.

After they had eaten, Pastor Fraser donned some hip waders and the deacons set up a bunch of white towels, white cotton choir-style robes, and bathrobes on a table next to the water. Nearby was a portable PA system. Pastor Fraser called for all the candidates for baptism to get ready while he waded out into Lake Whatcom, a wireless microphone on his head. Rebecca and Loretta, already in their swimsuits, joined the other candidates in putting on the white robes, completely covering their bodies down to their ankles. Then, they all lined up on the beach. Pastor Fraser gave a short sermon about baptism and explained its significance, and then called each person, one at a time, to come out to him in the water to be baptized.

"Rebecca Robinson, have you accepted Jesus Christ as your Lord and Savior?" Pastor Fraser asked as she stood in the water next to him.

"Yes, I have," she said into the microphone by his mouth.

"Then, upon your profession of faith, I baptize you in the name of the Father, the Son, and the Holy Spirit. We are buried with Him in baptism and rise to newness of life," he said, dipping her backward in the lake until she was fully submerged, and then he brought her back up again.

When she came up from the water, Rebecca never felt so wet in all her life, and the soaked white robe clung to her. But she also felt overjoyed to be showing the world that she was a Christian.

Everyone on the shore applauded when each candidate was baptized. Rebecca waded to the shore and was handed a towel and a bathrobe. She stood there drying off and watched Loretta take her turn. After Loretta had come up out of the water, it was clear to everyone that she was pregnant. Rebecca met her on the shore, and they embraced. After removing their robes, and drying off, each girl's boyfriend hugged her.

When the baptismal service was over, many people, including Scott, Rebecca, Sean, and Loretta went swimming in the lake. As the sun began to set, people picked over the leftovers and waited for the fireworks show. Scott and Rebecca, and Sean and Loretta, went to sit on the beach by a fire with the others in their youth group; they took turns setting off fireworks. They could see the lights of Bellingham across Lake Whatcom and all the individual fireworks displays around the lake. At ten o'clock the display on the barge began. All the couples snuggled for the next twenty minutes, as they watched the show to sounds of patriotic music blaring from speakers on the barge across the water. The sound of the display was thunderous as each shell went off. Rebecca could smell the sulfur smoke filling the air. Joyous applause roared from the park at the end of the show. Afterward, everyone packed up and went home.

Throughout the month of July, Rebecca and Loretta studied the books Pastor Jake gave them and asked God for wisdom. It was becoming more obvious to Rebecca that she really did love Scott. He was the one she wanted to marry. She searched her heart and honestly felt she could accept him as he was. Yes, she hoped he would be open to change where necessary, but even if he didn't change she was prepared to love him anyway. Did he feel the same way about her? Was he willing to make sacrifices for her welfare? Did he love her as Christ loves His Church? These were things she had to find out.

On August first, Rebecca and Loretta went to the Anderson estate for Scott's eighteenth birthday party. Sean and Scott played basketball with Daniel and the other guys in the youth group while Rebecca and Loretta sat by the pool and talked.

"I think Sean is definitely the one for me," Loretta said. "I've read all those books Pastor Jake gave us and really believe I love him. I want to be his wife. I want to do all that I can to make him happy."

"But how does he feel about you?" Rebecca asked. "Is he willing to serve you, too?"

"Yes, Sean has gone out of his way to help me during this pregnancy. He didn't have to do that. Especially since it's not his kid. What about Scott?"

"Lately, Scott has given up part of his Saturdays to help me stock the pantry at Rick's and take inventory without being paid. I think he just likes being around me. Of course, I like being with him too. It's really fun working together."

The guys returned from the basketball court and joined the girls for some birthday cake and ice cream.

"How would you ladies like to go on an end-of-summer picnic with Sean and me next Saturday, before school starts again?" Scott asked.

"You know you don't have to ask, of course we'll go with you," Rebecca said. "I'll see if Rick will give me that day off. I've enjoyed working with him in the kitchen this summer."

"We never want to take you for granted," Sean said.

"That's right. We'll pick you up at noon," Scott said.

On the following Friday, Scott and Sean had garment bags delivered to their girlfriends with Medieval princess dresses inside.

Sean had Loretta's specially tailored to accommodate her pregnancy. Scott put the following note with Rebecca's dress:

"Hey Princess, wear this dress to our special Medieval themed picnic tomorrow. See you tomorrow at noon for a day and 'knight' you'll never forget! Love, Scott."

Rebecca and Loretta both got "dolled up" in their princess dresses Saturday morning, and promptly at noon, a white Cinderella-style carriage with two stunning white horses pulled up in front of their homes. Both Scott and Sean climbed down from the carriage and went to their respective girlfriend's house dressed in chain mail and gleaming armor, which they'd rented from a costume shop.

"Greetings, Princess. Your carriage awaits you." Scott gave a single long stem red rose to Rebecca when she came out the door.

"Oh my Prince, this is too much," Rebecca said through her tears. "This is so romantic!"

The guys escorted their ladies to the carriage and helped them up into it before climbing up beside them. Then the coachman bid the horses to walk on, and they were off to the park. It was quite a spectacle as they rode through downtown Whatcom. When they arrived at the parking lot, Scott and Sean helped their dates down from the carriage.

"Look, Loretta, they've even made a flower-strewn path for us to walk on," Rebecca said.

"You guys have been busy this week," Loretta said.

Both couples walked hand in hand down the path to their special meadow where they found two medieval pavilions erected at each end, which afforded them some measure of privacy. Scott and Rebecca went to one tent, and Sean and Loretta went to the other. Inside the tent, Rebecca found a picnic lunch on a table with two chairs. The table was covered with a white linen table cloth. There were two fine china place settings and a silver candelabrum. Scott and Rebecca sat down at the table and began to eat, after giving thanks for the meal.

"You've really outdone yourself this time, my Prince."

"I wanted this day to be extra special because I'm leaving for Boston in a couple of weeks. I got accepted at MIT for their Aerospace Engineering program. I won't be back until Thanksgiving."

"Yes, and I'll miss you something awful."

"That's why I hope this picnic will take some of the sting out of my absence. I love you Rebecca, and I want to spend the rest of my life with you." Scott pulled out a dazzling engagement ring and fell to one knee. "Will you marry me, Princess?"

For a few seconds Rebecca was speechless, and then the momentous nature of the event hit her. She grabbed Scott and kissed him, tears gushing down her cheeks.

"I take it that's a 'yes.'"

"Yes! Yes! Of course, I'll marry you. How did you plan all this?"

Just then, they heard squeals of delight coming from the other tent.

"Does this mean what I think it means?" Rebecca asked Scott.

"Yes, it does. Sean and I planned to propose before we go off to college, and pooled our resources to pull it off. We both have your parents' blessing, and they agreed to keep mum until we proposed, with the understanding that we wouldn't get married until you both graduate from high school next year."

"This is awesome! Loretta and I were thinking about having a double wedding, assuming you guys wanted to marry us. But what about cooking school? I want to go to Le Cordon Bleu and study to become a chef."

"No problem. There's a Cordon Bleu in Cambridge, a few blocks from MIT. I have a cozy little apartment lined up already that's close to both schools. So, now you and Loretta can spend your senior year planning a wedding and applying for college. And if you're good, I'll try to get back here for your senior prom and graduation," Scott teased.

Loretta, followed by Sean, burst into their tent. Both girls squealed with delight as they showed each other their rings and jumped up and down, hugging each other. Sean fetched their food and chairs from the second tent so both couples could eat together. When the girls weren't looking, Scott sent a text to all their parents telling them the girls said, "Yes." Scott and Sean just sat back quietly during the afternoon as Rebecca and Loretta suggested ideas for their double wedding.

"You ladies can plan the wedding, but Scott and I will be planning our honeymoons," Sean remarked. "And I think you know, Loretta darlin', where I want to go."

"Ireland?" Loretta asked. "Oh yes, that would be wonderful!"

"And I'm thinking of a couple of places, Princess. You have a choice of a château in France or the Lalokai Resort in Maui."

"I choose Maui, my Prince, because it was there I first got to know you."

Scott's cell phone rang. "Hello, Daniel. Are you waiting for us in the parking lot? Okay, we'll be there soon. That, ladies and gentleman, is our ride. Shall we go? We can just leave this stuff. The caterer will come by after we leave and collect everything."

Both couples walked out to the parking lot hand in hand. Scott and Sean held up their new fiancés' hands, with the rings on their fingers, and Daniel produced a huge smile.

"Well, well, let me be the first to congratulate you all." Daniel shook both guys' hands and hugged the girls.

Scott and Sean helped the girls into the car, a tight fit with their princess dresses, and sat beside them. As they drove away, it soon became apparent they weren't going back to the girls' homes.

"Where are we going?" Loretta asked.

"Since you agreed to marry us, we have yet another surprise for you," Scott said. "We're going to my parents' estate for a joint engagement party. All our parents and some of our friends are already there."

"You think of everything, don't you? What would you guys do if we'd said, 'no'?" Rebecca teased.

"Oh, we would have just taken you home to an empty house and called your parents with the bad news," Sean retorted.

Daniel drove the car up next to the front door. Scott and Sean helped their future brides out and followed the butler into the living room and then to the balcony overlooking the courtyard below. He struck a small gong, and with a booming voice, the butler announced, "Ladies and gentlemen—our guests of honor have arrived!"

As Scott and Rebecca, Sean and Loretta, stood holding hands by the railing, applause and cheers erupted down below from their friends and family. The two couples then made their way downstairs to the party, and all the parents took tons of photos. Finally, after lots of hand shaking and hugs, Scott turned to Sean and said, "Let's get into something more comfortable. This armor is killing me."

The guys disappeared upstairs to Scott's room for about ten minutes and returned wearing black tuxedos, which resulted in more photos of the two couples.

"Your note was right Scott. This is a day and night I will never forget!"

"Good. Then we succeeded in creating a most memorable proposal."

"Mom and Dad, Loretta and I want to have a double wedding next June," Rebecca said.

"That's good dear, but we hope you'll get married at St. Paul's," Mrs. Robinson said.

"Only if Pastor Fraser can officiate at the wedding," Rebecca said.

"You all can have the reception here if you wish," Mrs. Anderson said.

"Where are you going for your honeymoon?" Mr. Anderson asked.

"That's classified!" Scott said. Everyone laughed.

The next day, their engagement was front page news in the *Whatcom Gazette*, but only because it was the most exciting thing they had to print that day. There was even a photo spread showing both couples in the carriage on Main Street, the pavilions in the park, and a shot of them standing on the balcony at the Anderson estate. Needless to say, that was one newspaper clipping that all the families kept for their scrapbooks. Rebecca and Loretta were totally stoked and anxious for June to come. Rebecca felt so blessed to be engaged to Scott.

To think. It all started with what she'd thought was a UFO.

Contact Information

To order additional copies of this book, please visit
www.redemption-press.com.
Also available on Amazon.com and BarnesandNoble.com
Or by calling toll free 1-844-2REDEEM.

CPSIA information can be obtained
at www.ICGtesting.com
Printed in the USA
LVHW012045180520
655844LV00002B/237